the
CARAMEL
CROW

A MEGAN MONTAIGNE MYSTERY

BOOKS by PAM STUCKY

FICTION

Mystery
Death at Glacier Lake
Final Chapter: A Megan Montaigne Mystery
A Conventional Murder: A Megan Montaigne Mystery
The Caramel Crow: A Megan Montaigne Mystery

Balky Point Adventures (MG/YA sci-fi)
The Universes Inside the Lighthouse
The Secret of the Dark Galaxy Stone
The Planet of the Memory Thieves

the Wishing Rock series (contemporary fiction) (novels with recipes)
Letters from Wishing Rock
The Wishing Rock Theory of Life
The Tides of Wishing Rock
From the Wishing Rock Kitchens: Recipes from the Series

NONFICTION

the Pam on the Map travel series (wit and wanderlust)
Pam on the Map: Iceland
Pam on the Map: Seattle Day Trips
Pam on the Map (Retrospective): Switzerland
Pam on the Map (Retrospective): Ireland

www.pamstucky.com

the
CARAMEL
CROW

A MEGAN MONTAIGNE MYSTERY

PAM STUCKY

Wishing Rock Press

Published in the United States by Wishing Rock Press.

Cover artwork by Madison Erin Mayfield
Cover design by Pam Stucky

ISBN (print): 978-1-940800-22-6
ISBN (ebook): 978-1-940800-23-3

www.wishingrockpress.com

for my book group:
Karen, Mike, Danae, and John
and sometimes
Angie, Sandy, Dori, and Tony

Almost 25 years now.
Everyone should be so lucky.

"Wherever your life ends, it is all there. The utility of living consists not in the length of days, but in the use of time; a man may have lived long, and yet lived but a little. Make use of time while it is present with you. It depends upon your will, and not upon the number of days, to have a sufficient length of life."

— *Michel de Montaigne, 1533–1592*

MAP OF EMERSON FALLS

(subject to reconstruction)

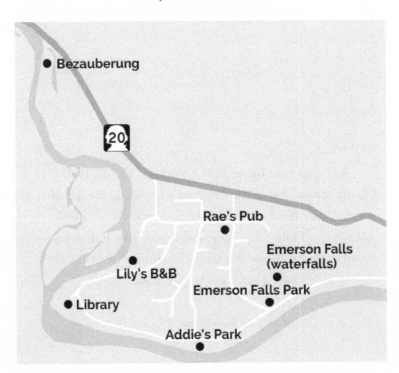

PROLOGUE

My mother was an alcoholic and a drug user. I loved her, until she died from an overdose, and I still love her, in the way you love someone who did their best and is now gone.

My father was absent, then semi-present, then absent. He wasn't in the picture for my first few years, but then he and my mom tried to work things out for a while when I was in my late single digits. Seven, eight, nine, ten.

They tried.

Neither of them was particularly spiritual, and neither of them was particularly around much. So I sort of got all my ideas about the world from just myself.

I don't really believe in an afterlife or any of that, but sometimes I wonder. Like, have you ever met someone, and you just *know* you already know them? I don't mean you've already met them. I mean your heart, your soul, just recognizes them. Instantly.

I like to think of it like this: all of time is happening all at once. The past, present, and future—everything is happening at the same time. And the future version of me, who already knows a person that current-me hasn't yet met, suddenly flips through the veil, that's what I've heard it called, the veil. The veil of time. That future version of me filters through the veil in my mind and I realize that *I know this person already* and that they're supposed to be in my life. You see them and you know.

That's how it was with Joel.

We met in a tattoo parlor. He was in the chair, getting a tattoo. I walked in to get my first. I was nineteen, and I was early because I'd found parking right away, which never happens. So I figured it was a sign: I was supposed to get this tattoo.

Joel was sitting in the chair, just quietly watching the tattoo artist as she carved into his arm. It felt reassuring to see him so calm. A person wouldn't be that calm if it hurt, would they? But he had other tattoos already. He was used to this. It was a badge of strength.

He heard the door open and looked up to see who had walked in. When he saw me, he looked at me with a smile like he'd been expecting me all day, and where had I been? Like he knew me already, too. That was the moment. I saw through the veil of time, and future-me told present-me that this guy was important.

"Are you here to get a tattoo?" he said from across the room, his smile broad, like his shoulders. "Or are you here to make all my dreams come true?"

Those dark eyes, almost black. A flop of dark brown hair across his forehead.

My heart skipped.

"Maybe both," I said. I had no idea where the words came from. I wasn't that bold.

His eyes flashed, filled with universes. He scanned me up and down, slowly, like I was an assignment and he was studying hard. It was a summer day, hot. I was in a tank top, red, tight. Shorts, denim, cutoff. Flipflops. My plain brown hair, dyed almost black, tied back in a ponytail. He could see a lot of my skin. All of it bare.

"First tattoo?" he said, raising an eyebrow. That eyebrow, I would come to learn, spoke volumes. If a picture is worth a thousand words, his eyebrow was an encyclopedia. His mouth was asking about my tattoo, but his eyebrow wanted to know what I was doing later.

A picture of his mouth, by the way, is in the dictionary next to the word "luscious." Where most people have lips, he had invitations. I wanted to RSVP immediately: *yes*.

"First tattoo," I said. I stood with my lips open, breathing in the cool air-conditioned air, looking at his eyes. Dark brown eyes, endless, like the inside of that wardrobe that would take you to Narnia. To other worlds.

"Come sit," he said, nodding his head at an empty chair beside him.

The tattoo artist continued with her work. She said nothing, stared intently at his arm where she was working, but the slight crinkle at the corner of her eyes, the slightly raised corner of one side of her mouth, let me know she was aware of what was happening.

Of course, how could she not be? I was afraid the electricity between him and me might spark a fire in that room.

"Hold my hand in case I get scared," he said, as he held my eyes, locked, no key.

I held his free hand and we sat there saying nothing. He turned to watch the tattoo artist as she finished up. All three of us, eyes riveted to his arm, but my whole soul was in the palm of his hand. The quiet was as thick as a down jacket on a hot day; the only sound was the buzz of the tattoo machine.

A tattoo pen, I thought, writing my future.

When Joel was done, the tattoo artist cleaned up and then set me into the chair.

"I'll hold your hand," Joel said, sitting in the seat I'd warmed.

I pulled a paper out of my shorts pocket. I unfolded it to show him the tattoo I was going to get, then gave it to the artist. I pointed to my right ankle. "Here."

"Why not…" he said, then paused. He reached toward my chest and lightly, like a feather, touched the skin at the top of my left breast. "…here?" He touched me only for a second, a millisecond, but his fingers blazed fire through my body. "On your heart?"

I had to remind myself to breathe.

I looked at the tattoo artist and raised my own eyebrows.

She shrugged. It didn't matter to her.

I nodded.

"You'll need to … move the tank top out of the way," she said.

Bold future-me swept in again. I crossed my arms in front of me and pulled my tank top over my head. The yellow polka-dot bra I was wearing wasn't fancy, but it covered as much as a bikini top would. In a pinch, I could have used it as a bikini top. What was the difference, really? Marketing? How long it took to dry?

I gave the tank top to Joel to hold. He settled it into his lap and looked at me again with that eyebrow, those lips. Told me an entire story with his eyebrow and lips.

He reached for my hand.

I leaned back in the chair.

When the tattoo artist set the pen to my chest and turned the machine on, I gasped, closed my eyes, and bit my lip. Joel squeezed my hand.

Forty minutes later, we were eating ice cream by the lake. He reached out, held his fingers just millimeters above my chest. The bandage still covered the tattoo but I could feel his heat radiating from his hand.

"So I should know your name," he said, looking at the bandage like he could see through it, straight to my heart.

"Branwen," I said. "Bran."

"I'm Joel," he said. "Just Joel." He smiled.

"Nice to meet you, Joel." I caught a drip of chocolate ice cream that was escaping down the side of my cone.

Joel watched my tongue. Then he said a few things with that eyebrow again.

He believed in waiting. Four very long weeks later, he kissed me for the first time.

It was after dinner.

"There's a bread crumb on your lip," he said, eyes on my mouth.

I licked my lips. "Did I get it?" I asked.

"No," he said, and he leaned in and touched his lips to mine, the softest lips I'd ever felt. Invitation received. He tasted like destiny.

Three months later, we got an apartment together.

A month after that, I found out he was up to his eyeballs in a drug ring.

Four months after that, I started trying to get him to change his life.

A month after that, he agreed.

Two weeks after that, they killed him in front of my eyes.

ONE

A light breeze blew Candace's dry, bleached-blonde hair into her eyes as she lowered her binoculars. She glanced sideways at her husband with a deep internal sigh. The advice in one of the relationship self-help books she'd been reading lately popped into her head: *Act as if. Act as if* she loved him. *Act as if* they had the relationship she longed for. *Act as if* the marriage wasn't a sham from the start, that it hadn't her plan all along for him to die early and leave his fortune to her to spend as she wished.

"See anything, darling?" she said sweetly, pulling the irritation from her breath just before it slipped out.

Giles was oblivious. Giles was almost giddy. He scanned the horizon steadily, switching from binoculars to naked eyes and back. A delighted, preoccupied grin stretched across his face. He didn't respond.

"Anything?" Candace tried again, feigning cheerfulness. When she'd married Giles thirteen years ago, him at age fifty-two and her at thirty-four, she'd been sure he loved his job so much he would never quit. That he would just keep bringing in the six-digit income until he died one day in the hospital, surrounded by his drugs and his patients. When she'd first met Giles—targeted him, really, but that was just a technicality—she'd been working at a travel company that specialized in birding tours. She'd met all sorts of men who had far too much money for their own good; after all; who could afford to spend thousands of dollars chasing down rare birds each year? Giles had been handsome, and sweet, and lonely, and he'd tipped her extra when she managed to get him onto a sold-out excursion.

Bullseye, Candace had thought.

On discovering his line of work, she'd taken a week to learn how to spell "anesthesiologist." To impress him. Charm him. And charmed he was. Giles was a smart man but a simple man, and at fifty-two he'd been five years out of a twenty-year marriage that had ended when his wife died in a tragic car accident. All he'd wanted was to be cared for. To have someone at home to make him dinner and decide what to do with all the money he brought in. When a sweet, pretty, young blonde came along, his head was turned. When she knew how to spell anesthesiologist, well, that nearly sealed the deal right there. He wooed her. She played hard to get, just so he wouldn't think the relationship had been her idea. She was not smart, but she was coy. She saw what she wanted and she went for it.

After they were married, slowly at first, Candace had stopped pretending. Yes, it would have been nice to have real love, but she'd bagged her kill. She'd gotten what she wanted. Giles was committed to his work and wasn't paying attention anyway. So long as dinner was on the table when he got home, he was happy, and the local caterer was happy to help with that. What point was there in working harder than she needed to? But as it turned out, Giles didn't love his job as much as she'd thought, and he retired on turning sixty-five. What's more, he wanted her attention again. At first she balked. After not too long, he gave up and pulled away, and she then panicked. Dollar signs in her eyes, flying away with him out the door. So she started pretending again.

Act as if.

"Do you think maybe it's gone?" Candace said. "Maybe we were too late." Giles was not, and never had been, a hard-core birder. But with his retirement, his passion for birding was rising like a phoenix from the flames. Candace's job with the tour company had been a job, but she'd always let Giles think she loved the flitty things as much as he did. Now he wanted her to travel on birding adventures with him, and it was all she could do not to tape skewers to the back of her binoculars and poke her eyes out.

Giles turned his attention to her without actually looking at her, like his aura was looking in her direction though his eyes were not. "We'll just stay a little longer, shall we? It's a *five*, Candy. A rare swallow-tail gull, here in the United States when it's supposed to be down in the Galapagos. On the rarity list, it's a *five*. The highest is six. Six is birds that are extinct." Birders from all over the country, literally, had flown here to see this bird. For the birders, this was a big deal.

Candace breathed in sharply through her nose, hoping the extra oxygen would cull her boredom. "So the only thing more rare than a swallow-tail gull in Edmonds, Washington, would be an extinct bird in Edmonds, Washington?" She forced a smile, thinking the smile would add congeniality to her tone.

Giles nodded indulgently. "Yes. An extinct bird flying into the United States would probably cause more of a stir." His eyes were still focused on the endless sky. Other gulls, mostly common glaucous gulls, cried out as they wheeled through the sky, their eyes laser-focused on any food the throng of birders might drop. A half of a sandwich, untended, could disappear in an instant.

Candace lifted the ends of her lips but could not bring herself to carry the smile up to her eyes.

"Oh, say, there's Lester," Giles said. He raised a hand to wave at another older man who was walking their way, and the handsome, weathered man returned the gesture.

Candace pursed her lips. Lester Heybrook was not a man she wanted to see. He was, in fact, a man she'd rather forget. He brought bad memories with him. But Giles didn't know that.

Lester nodded at Giles, slowly, then added a nod to Candace as almost an afterthought. He followed Giles's gaze out toward the sea. "Did you see it?" he asked.

"Candy thinks maybe it's gone," Giles said, shaking his head. "I can't believe we were too late. There have only been a couple of these in the United States, ever."

"Alive anyway," Candace said.

Giles acknowledged her words with a nod, but it was clear he wasn't paying attention.

Lester tilted his own binoculars up to his eyes. "I think you're right. It's moved on. Came up from south of here, closer to Seattle, but no one's seen it for the last few hours. Such is the nature of birds." He put the binoculars down. "They fly away."

"Oh!" Giles said, letting his binoculars fall to his chest, secured by a strap around his neck. "My phone!" He pulled the buzzing device out of his jacket pocket and squinted at it, then pulled a pair of reader glasses out of another pocket. "An alert!" he said, and his eyes gleamed as he tapped through.

"Rare bird?" said Lester, his interest piqued. He pulled out his own phone and started tapping.

"Yes!" said Giles. He paused to read. "Leucistic crow." His excitement faded just a bit. "Well, it's no swallow-tail gull, but it looks like we've lost our chance with this one." Giles looked up at the sky one last time but he had to admit the celebrated gull was gone. He handed the phone to Candace to show her the alert. "Fancy a side-trip?"

Candace was on the verge of needing reading glasses herself, but she would never admit it. "Leucistic crow … Emerson Falls, Washington." She stared at the phone for a minute without saying anything. "Emerson Falls. Where's that?" She switched to the map app and searched. "About two hours northeast of here," she said. She then read from a website: "The small town of Emerson Falls is located in a curve of the Skagit River, near the entrance to the North Cascades National Park. It is an excellent recreational area, known for its spectacular waterfalls, as well as hiking, river rafting, eagle watching, and other bird viewing. A local mansion was recently renovated into a library with a convention center in its lower level; the vast garages were reconstructed into a new theater scheduled to open with its first production soon." Candace handed the phone back to her husband. "I think it sounds like a lovely place for a mini-vacation. Maybe you can see some eagles and owls," she said. "Or maybe we'll find that cute one we both love, that golden-crowned kinglet."

The little bird was cute, Candace thought, but to say she actually cared about a golden-crowned kinglet was a bit of a stretch. *Act as if.*

Lester was staring at the listing on his own phone, with an expression on his face that seemed more like a wall than a disclosure. "Well, well" he said finally. "A leucistic crow. It's been a while. Maybe I'll go, too."

Candace raised her eyebrows. Lester was a serious birder. He'd even tried for the Big Year a few times—the birding world's competition to see who could spot the most birds in one year—winning once and coming close twice. That had been long ago, and he wasn't as avid a birder anymore, it seemed. Still, an odd-colored crow seemed an unlikely draw for the old man. Candace glanced at Giles to see if he, too, was surprised, but her husband had his binoculars up to his eyes again, scanning the beach one last time for a glimpse of the coveted gull.

Act as if, Candace told herself, and she patted Giles on the shoulder as lovingly as she could manage. *Act as if.*

TWO

"Two hundred ninety-six!" Carol Louis-Lewis (née Louis) declared, looking at her phone. She leaned over to show her wife, Betty Louis-Lewis (née Lewis). "Two hundred ninety six! Can you believe it?"

Betty shook her head. "That's something. Still at least a hundred short of that eagle picture I posted. But not bad."

"What's that?" Megan Montaigne, Library Director in Emerson Falls, Washington, was folding chairs and leaning them against one of the shelves. She'd recently started a library book group, and the evening's discussion had just wrapped up. The only people still in the library were those lingering to gossip—which, of course, included Carol and Betty. They'd lived in the area as long as anyone could remember, and in their retirement had picked up numerous activities that kept them active.

Lily Bell, Megan's best friend and owner of the local B&B, craned her neck over Carol's shoulder to look at her phone. She saw Carol had the Instagram app open, with a light-colored bird filling the screen.

"A bird?" Lily said. "I don't recognize it. What kind is that?"

"It's a leucistic crow," Carol said proudly, handing the phone to Lily so she could get a better look. "Leucistic means it has a genetic mutation that gives it abnormal coloring. Leucistic birds have varying amounts of pigment. You can see that this one is sort of almond colored."

"Is it albino?" Megan asked, looking over Lily's shoulder.

"No," Carol said. "It's different from albino. You see its eyes, they'd be red if it were albino."

"Some leucistic birds are quite white, though," Betty said, nodding.

"Some are quite white," Carol confirmed. "This one has a lovely bronze to it. I posted the picture on my Instagram. People can't get enough of it. There's a woman who's always posting photos of a leucistic hummingbird that comes to her yard. You'd think she gave birth to the bird herself, the way she dotes on it. But I've never seen a leucistic crow before." Her pride in her photo beamed out of her every pore.

"One of my eagle pictures has more likes, though," Betty repeated, lips pressed thin, but a twinkle in her eye showed she, too, was pleased with the picture, and the number of likes it was getting. "The one where it's just caught that fish and is rising away from the river."

"Oh, Betty," Carol said, gently patting Betty's knee. "That's right. That eagle photo does have more likes. It's lovely. Remember, it's not a competition."

Betty raised an eyebrow and shot Megan a look that said: *it's a competition.*

"That's stunning," Lily said, handing the phone to Megan. "And maybe that explains the calls I've been getting at the B&B today. People wanting to know if this is the town where 'the crow' is. I didn't recognize the word 'leucistic' so it didn't register in my brain, but now I'm sure that's what they're saying. I have some people incoming, looking to find your crow."

"It's beautiful," said Megan. "Where did you take this?"

"Out by the falls," Carol said with a sigh of pleasure. The falls she was referring to were Emerson Falls, which was actually a series of waterfalls with multiple drops and turns, for which the town was named. Megan handed the phone back to her, and Carol checked the likes again. "Two hundred ninety-nine!" she said. "This is my best yet."

Lily started packing up the leftover perfectly decorated cookies she'd brought for the group. At the last meeting there hadn't been any leftovers—she was one of the best bakers in town, and occasionally helped with catering at local events. Therefore, this time, Lily had made a double batch. Even so, there were only a few left.

"Leave me one?" Megan said, grabbing for a cookie shaped like a book, its icing so smooth it made Megan want to pet it.

Lily smiled and pulled three cookies out of the container, handing one each to Megan, Betty, and Carol. "You know, I've been researching the history of Emerson Falls for that book I want to write. I've been reading the diaries of our town's dear founding father, Chester Robert Emerson. I swear he once mentioned seeing a crow that he said was the wrong color. If I remember right, it scared the dickens out of him. He thought it was a bad omen. I'll have to go back and check."

"Interesting. I've never even heard of such a thing," Megan said. "Leucistic." She rolled the word around on her tongue. "Leucistic. A leucistic crow."

The only two chairs left to be put away were those that Betty and Carol were sitting in. Megan was in no rush. The book group had only met a few times but already she found it was one of her favorite nights of the month. Not just the chance to talk about books, which she loved and could never get enough of, but also the camaraderie of like-minded souls, curious about the world and everything in it. While she was tired and the day had been long, she found she didn't want the evening to end.

"Are you sure it's a crow?" Megan continued. "I've never heard of a crow that color."

"Darling, I know crows. As I said, it's rare," Carol said, though it seemed she enjoyed Megan's doubt. It made her photo all the more special, if someone couldn't believe it was real. "And your Lily here said Chester Emerson himself wrote about one."

Lily nodded. "I'm sure he did. Now I'm going to fret about that until I can find that passage again. I wonder if your crow is related to his crow? Whether the trait is passed on genetically?"

"Well," said Carol sighing, "I can't say for sure. But I have read that leucism in animals is much more appreciated by us humans than by others in their species. They're more likely to be rejected by their own kind. And I suppose if you're rejected, you're less likely to mate and pass the trait on. Still, every one of us is, technically, a mutation." She shrugged, then grinned to herself as she looked at the picture again. "Three hundred! Three hundred likes. Imagine that. I'm going to have to take that old crow some nuts."

Lights from a car in the parking lot outside shone in through the large library windows. "Rehearsal must be over," Megan said. Indeed, it looked like a handful of cars were starting to leave the lot. The library had started its life as a mansion, which later was donated to the town by its previous owner after his divorce and renovated into its current use. The main level held the library, but the fourteen-thousand-square-foot home was far too large for the tiny town's library needs. Therefore, they'd converted the lower level into conference rooms, and the upper level had been made into a living space for the Library Director, Megan. Megan thought that so long as the Library Director got to live in this spectacular space, she would never want to leave. The building was situated on a gorgeous, dramatic curve along the Skagit River, and every night and every morning she went out onto her balcony overlooking the water and sent out a word of thanks.

When the building had first been converted, the library board hadn't been sure what to do with the huge garage area. Eventually they'd fallen on the idea of converting it into a theater. The theater's very first show was just about to open, and the buzz all over Emerson Falls was about the play and the newly renovated space. Tomorrow night would be the dress rehearsal, and then Friday, opening night. Having the theater next door had already brought so much energy and excitement to the library, and Megan was as excited as the theater staff, cast, and crew. She'd offered to host a celebration party after the first show, downstairs in the convention rooms. The party was open to everyone, and it sounded like everyone in town was planning to come. What with all the other plans Megan was thinking of to make the library into a community gathering space, she was practically humming with anticipation.

The front door to the library, still unlocked for the evening, flung wide open, letting in a gust of fresh fall air. With it came a young woman, mid-twenties, her dark hair flying wildly with the wind.

"Hey, Bridget," Megan said, smiling. She nodded at Lily. "Grab a cookie before Lily escapes with all the leftovers."

Bridget Hill, stage manager for the theater's first production, looked toward Lily and put up a slim hand. "No, thanks. Tatum brought a ton of snacks to rehearsal. I think I'm half carrot sticks right now."

"Are you guys ready for opening night?" Megan asked. "Ready to climb every mountain?" The theater manager, Jace Fleming, had decided a familiar show would draw a bigger crowd than something new and edgy, no matter how good. Plus, he'd explained, with so many characters, they'd get more "butts in seats," as he'd put it: friends and family coming to see their loved ones on stage. For the first production, *The Sound of Music* would fill the theater.

"The hills are alive," Bridget said with a smirk. "Hey, a favor, do you have a spare power cord? Someone spilled water all over one of ours and it's fried. I'll try to get to the store tomorrow but it would be nice to have a backup. Everything's a bit crazy over there right now."

"Of course," Megan said. "I'll bring one by first thing tomorrow, how's that?"

"That would be great," Bridget said. She nodded quietly at Carol, Betty, and Lily, and left without another word.

When the door was shut behind her, Betty spoke up. "That girl is unusual," she said, shaking her head.

"She's perfectly sweet," Lily objected. "What do you mean?" She sealed the lid on the cookie container and released the extra air.

"Anti-social," Carol said. "Always alone. We once invited her along on a birding adventure. Then on a bike ride or hike. Then we asked her to come for dinner. Trying to be good neighbors, you see. She lives two houses away from us and never seems to have any friends over. So we were trying to be nice. But she refuses every time." Carol sniffed, and Betty echoed the sound.

"We've given up trying, to be honest," Betty said. "We tried long enough."

Megan stifled a smile. Although Carol claimed they were trying to be good neighbors, more likely they were being at least a little bit nosy. They couldn't stand not knowing everything going on in town. A person who wasn't an open book was irresistible to them. As far as Bridget's reticence, it might be the company, Megan thought, not the activities. She loved Carol and Betty, but they could be an acquired taste. They were not subtle, and they didn't hold back their opinions. Bridget had always been perfectly nice to Megan in the library. Not quite standoffish, but also not unfriendly. "Maybe she's just shy," Megan said. "Or introverted."

"The other people in the theater seem to like her," Lily said. "I've seen her and Jace at Rae's a few times." Rae's Pub was the local restaurant, run by Rae Norris. Rae couldn't be bothered to have a menu, and her customers loved it. Just like at home, they got what was placed in front of them, and the food never failed to be anything but delicious. Rae was a superb chef, and what's more, she knew the favorite meal of every person in town and would take requests, occasionally, if she liked you. Megan and Lily, as well as most of the town, hung out there regularly.

"How long has Bridget lived here?" Megan asked. "Like a couple of years?"

"Oh, I think at least three, isn't it?" Lily said.

"Three and a half," Betty said. "Moved here just after all the eagle frenzy was over three years ago." The Skagit River area, where Emerson Falls was located, was famous for prolific eagle watching in the winter, culminating in a month-long festival in January.

"I'm just saying there's something about her," Carol said.

Megan simply nodded. Having transplanted herself to the area many years back, she knew only too well how long it had been before anyone considered her anything other than an outsider. She made a mental note to invite Bridget up to her balcony for coffee sometime, to get to know her better. Bridget might well be interested in more friends, but perhaps closer to her own age.

"Well," Carol said, standing and folding her chair against the others. "We'd better get going. Betty promised me she'd watch a home improvement show with me, and I am holding her to it. Lily, if any of your guests need guides to take them to see that crow, tell them we'll do it for twenty dollars a head." She nodded to show she meant it. Then, the Louis-Lewises waved goodbye and were out the door quickly.

"Speaking of dinner," Megan said, looking at Lily. "I'm famished. Want to drop by Rae's with me?"

Lily looked up at the ceiling, seeming to run through her head what her obligations were for the evening. "I think I can do that. Steve is watching the B&B, and he's got a game he wanted to watch tonight. I'll tell him to heat something up for himself. Sure." She quickly texted her husband. "Okay. Let's go!"

Fifteen minutes later, Megan and Lily were sitting at a table at Rae's. They'd caught the tail end of the dinner crowd, and as they waited for their meals, the room slowly emptied. This was the way Megan liked it. She thought again of Bridget. Carol and Betty were extroverts, Betty more so than Carol. They were both outgoing, outspoken, in the middle of the action, and would never turn down an invitation. To them, Bridget undoubtedly seemed strange. Megan, however, understood the need to have her own space, and knew that Carol and Betty's direct attitude could lead a quieter person to shy away. Even here at Rae's, Megan always enjoyed seeing the people she knew; but still, she enjoyed the place more when it was less busy. When she could breathe and enjoy the time she was spending with the people she truly cared about. Like Lily, and Rae.

Soon, Rae appeared from behind the swinging kitchen doors, carrying a platter of hot, delicious food. "Gruyere on market toast and tomato bisque tonight," Rae said, placing the plates and full bowls in front of her guests.

"Oh my gosh," Lily said, eyes wide. "This looks perfect. Is there a better meal than grilled cheese and tomato soup?"

"*Gruyere on market toast and tomato bisque*," Megan corrected, winking at Rae. "Why so fancy?" She picked up half a sandwich, dipped it in the soup, and took a bite. "Yummmmmm."

Rae shrugged, hands on hips. "I got a bee in my bonnet. Felt like changing it up a bit." She tucked a stray lock of her white-blonde hair behind her ear.

"Felt like charging the tourists more, you mean?" Megan laughed. Lately, Emerson Falls seemed to be getting more business. The library had recently hosted a travel convention, and Megan thought she could see the fruits of all their labor. More people seemed to be dropping by their small town every day.

"Eh," said Rae. "If they want to pay an extra two dollars for fancy Swiss cheese, who am I to deny their tastebuds the pleasure?" She winked and headed back to the kitchen.

The restaurant's outside door opened. A young man blinked his way inside, his eyes adjusting to the dim interior light. He wore a black leather jacket and jeans with heavy boots, and a messenger bag over his shoulder. His dark hair looked wind-blown and his cheeks were rosy. His demeanor was as disheveled as he was. He looked around the room as if he wasn't sure where he was.

Megan gave Lily a glance, then shrugged. The young man saw them, and came over.

"Hello, ladies," he said, eyeing their soup and sandwiches with envy. "Sorry to bother you. I've had a bit of car trouble. Is there a mechanic in town?"

Megan laughed. "Not in this town. A couple of towns over is your best bet."

The man sighed. "Okay. How far is that?"

Megan thought. "About five miles," she said. "Is your car drivable?"

The man ran a hand through his hair. "Not so much," he said. "I ran over something in the road and my car conked out." He shook his head. "Another driver helped me push it to the shoulder, then I walked here." He looked at his watch. "I'm guessing even two towns over the shop is already closed. Do you think it'll be safe there for the night?"

"If it's fully on the shoulder, it should be," Megan said.

"Yeah, we got it all the way off," he said. "I suppose no chance there's a hotel here I can stay at tonight?"

"Well, there you're in luck. This here is Lily. She runs the B&B a few blocks away," Megan said.

The man's face brightened and he looked at Lily like she was a charm. "This is my lucky day indeed. You have a room available tonight miss?"

Lily smiled. "We definitely do. Let me get my meal packed to go and we'll get you settled." She trotted to the kitchen to get a to-go container from Rae.

Megan looked the young man over. The color in his cheeks had calmed down and he seemed calmer himself, now that his crisis was at least postponed. "Lily makes the best breakfast anywhere, and her B&B is gorgeous," she said to the man. "You've had a lucky misfortune. She and her husband, Steve, will take good care of you." She wasn't sure why she'd mentioned Steve, but something in her felt the need to let this man know Lily was not alone. "I'm Megan. Megan Montaigne. I'm the Library Director here."

"Simon Nash," the man said, shaking Megan's hand. "Nice to meet you. Where is 'here,' by the way?"

"Emerson Falls," Megan said. "If you have to be stuck somewhere, you couldn't be stuck anywhere better. What brings you out our way tonight?"

"Wanderlust," Simon said, half his mouth turning up in a cheesy grin out of a seventies sitcom. "Just pure wanderlust. Craving for the road. I heard Highway 20 was one of the country's best scenic roads. I'm between jobs and I had a hankering to go somewhere so I headed out."

"Where were you headed to tonight?" Megan asked. "Were you expected somewhere? Do you need to make a call?"

"I guess I was headed here," Simon said, running a hand over his hair again. "As fate would have it, Emerson Falls is my destiny."

Megan nodded. A free spirit, she thought. She'd met the type before. Some people knew exactly where they wanted to go. Other people only knew when they got there.

Lily returned with her food wrapped up, and handed a bag to Simon, as well. "My treat. A very special gruyere on market toast and tomato bisque. We want our visitors to feel welcome, even when they hadn't planned to visit." She beamed. Lily always beamed, Megan thought. Lily was light and sunshine and kindness.

Simon beamed in return. "Grilled cheese and tomato soup!" he said. "The best meal there is. Thank you!"

"The B&B is just a few blocks from here," Lily said. "If you can walk a bit more, we can walk."

"You lead, I'll follow," Simon said. He swept his arm forward, inviting Lily to show him the way.

Lily winked at Megan and headed toward the door, followed by Simon. As she opened the door, someone on the other side pushed it in, startling the people on both sides.

"Oh!" said Lily, backing into Simon, who hadn't backed up, almost knocking him over.

"I'm sorry!" said Bridget simultaneously. Her hand flew protectively to the man behind her, Jace Fleming, the theater manager. Her eyes moved from Lily to Simon. She blinked and moved away quickly.

"Goodnight!" Lily called after Bridget and Jace, who had turned and waved at Lily as he followed Bridget.

Simon's eyes trailed after Bridget appreciatively. "Emerson Falls is looking good so far," he said quietly.

Lily shook her head and waved back at Megan.

Megan pulled out her phone. *Text me when you're home safe,* she texted at Lily.

A few seconds later, her phone vibrated with an incoming text. *Will do, worrywart. X*

Megan finished her own sandwich, watching Bridget and Jace in their booth, trying to see if there was any special connection there. Nothing was obvious, but she knew that didn't mean anything. Besides which, her mind was preoccupied with another thought.

It was almost eight o'clock. The sun had already gone down. There were not a whole lot of towns on this part of the highway, and even fewer farther on.

If Simon had been out sightseeing, exactly where had he been going at this time of night?

THREE

"Hello, autumn sky," Megan mumbled toward her window from her bed the next morning as she awoke. Her bedroom, on the top floor of the old mansion that was now the library, had a balcony that looked out over the Skagit River rushing by below. Having no neighbors or buildings across the river from her bedroom, Megan kept the curtains open while she slept so she could watch the night sky. Whether a clear night with countless stars, or a stormy night with rain pounding against the glass, she loved watching and being immersed in nature's moods. And she loved waking up to a crisp autumn sky. "Nothing like the light of fall," she said as she stepped out onto the balcony. The angle of sunshine from the rising sun never failed to enchant her.

"I think a nice morning walk is in order," Megan said to the gurgling river below the balcony. The sound of the water was calling out to her, inviting her to walk along its banks. She needed to get the power cord to Bridget, but the theater crew would not be in the building until after noon. Her own job at the library also didn't start until noon; the library board couldn't afford to keep the library open full time just yet, though Megan was proud that finances had improved the last few months. Others in town were starting to see the library as she saw it: not just a building with books, but a town centerpiece, a place for people to gather. Money was coming in, and the community was growing.

Megan slipped into workout clothes and skipped downstairs and out the back door, which was the entrance for the library's living quarters. She stopped just outside, turned her face to the sun, and stood, eyes closed, like a sunflower basking in the warm rays. For several long moments, she soaked in the life-giving light and heat, taking it into her body and soul like sustenance. Once she was full, she took off at a brisk pace along the riverfront trail. One of her favorite spaces.

It was a popular trail for walks and runs, but the day was still young and she only encountered a couple of locals on the path. At about the halfway point between the library and Emerson Falls Park, she came to Addie's Park. Officially it was the Adeline Emerson Memorial Park, named for the first wife of the town's founder. Megan always felt Addie's presence there, somehow. Or maybe she just felt the presence of the person she thought Addie would have been. Megan hadn't known her, after all. She'd died young, not long after the town was founded, nearly a century and a half ago. Megan paused and contemplated the passing of time, the passing of Addie's life. Surely, at some point, the young woman and mother of six—the sixth being the cause of her own death—had stood in this same spot. Surely, Addie had, at some point, pondered the beauty of the site. Even as difficult as her life must have been, surely Addie had stopped, at some point, and turned her face to the sun.

Or had she? We make up stories about who people are, Megan thought, but maybe those stories told us more about ourselves than about the other. No matter how we try, we can never be anything but the center of our own universe. No matter how we try, our viewpoint can never be anything but our own. Megan tried to imagine being twenty-seven, mother of five, pregnant, wife of a powerful man building a new town on the banks of a river in a remote forest at the far edge of the country. Before running water and refrigeration were commonplace. Before modern medicine and vaccines. Not before libraries, Megan thought with a smile, but it was unlikely there had been any nearby. This would have been an isolated spot, a lonely existence, more than a hundred years before the road from east to west across the mountains was built. This town would have been near the end of the line, with just the wild and mostly impassable mountains and forests beyond. Megan imagined Addie, pregnant and twenty-seven and standing on the shores of this extraordinary river, face turned to the sun, the world and all of life seemingly spread before her, and not knowing her time was now numbered in days, not years.

That could be any of us, Megan thought. Almost none of us knows which day will our last.

"Carpe diem," she whispered to the bench at Addie's Park, and she walked quickly onward to the falls.

As always, Megan could hear the falls before she could see them. Of all the forms of water, Megan loved waterfalls the best. The sound felt like a beacon, guiding her way home. She smiled and quickened her step as she wound her way through the trails of the park. When she got to the main falls, she stopped abruptly. Of course it was a public park, and people were there all the time, but in the morning usually she could find herself alone. Today, however, a man stood there, staring at the falls, leaning against the railing, binoculars hanging loose on his chest. Megan's mind quickly flipped to images of the actor Paul Newman in his later years. This man had a similar look: chiseled features, fit with lean muscle, strikingly handsome, even from the side. His skin was tanned and his hair was light, in a way that hair and skin almost blended together. Though she imagined he might look young for his age, Megan guessed the man to be in his mid-sixties. Whoever he was, she'd never met him.

Whether because of the sound of the water or the sound of his own thoughts, he didn't hear her approach. Megan walked around in front of him, hoping not to startle him.

"Hello," Megan said.

The man turned his face to her, and his eyes matched the picture Megan had built: piercingly blue, a mix of light and dark blues that held her captive. Megan wondered what this man must have looked like when he was younger. She bet he'd had his share of women. Or men, if he'd preferred.

His smile was slow but honest, tinged with something Megan couldn't place. Excitement, maybe. Anticipation. "Hello," he said, and he offered nothing more.

For a moment, Megan was tempted to jump into a conversation, make the man feel welcome in what she considered part of her home. But his calm demeanor made her pause. Silent companionship was underrated. She leaned on the railing a few feet away from him, and turned her face to the waterfall, closing her eyes and absorbing the spray in the same way she'd greeted the sun. She stood like that for almost a minute, letting the mist wash over her like gratitude. Eventually, she opened her eyes again, and found the man watching her.

"You like water," he said, smiling.

Limbal ring, Megan thought. She remembered someone once told her that the outer ring of the iris of the eye, the part at the edge of the circle just before the whites of the eyes, was called the limbal ring. This man's limbal rings were dark blue, standing in stark contrast to the lighter, brighter, ocean blue of the main part of his iris. His limbal rings mesmerized her and she almost couldn't look away. Finally, she found her words again.

"I do like water," she said. "Do you?"

He blinked, thinking deeply on the question. "I like water," he said, "but I also like air."

Megan found herself breathing deeply, unintentionally. "Well, we need both," she said. The clean scent of the falls filled her.

"We *are* both," the man said. His voice was deep, aged but smooth.

The way he spoke, eyes attached to hers like a lifeline, Megan felt he *saw* her. She couldn't help but notice how much time he took with each answer. Was he slow? Or just measured?

She held out her hand, unsure whether he would return the gesture. "I'm Megan," she said. "Are you new in town?"

The man reached out his own hand, but instead of shaking Megan's hand, he held it. Briefly, not so long that it became weird, but long enough that the warmth of his rough hand left a residual imprint.

"Lester," he said. "Just visiting."

Megan suddenly remembered Carol's Instagram photo from the night before. "Are you looking for the crow?" she said, pointing to the man's binoculars. The caps were still on the ends, probably to keep the lenses from getting wet.

His smile spread. "Yes," he nodded. "Yes, I am. The caramel crow."

"The caramel crow?" Megan said, puzzled. This phrase was new.

"The lady at the bed and breakfast. She said the man who built this town referred to leucistic crows as caramel crows."

"Oh!" Megan said, pieces of the puzzle falling into the place. "Lily! She must have gone back to her history books and found what she was looking for. The woman who posted the Instagram photo told us about the leucistic crow last night, and Lily—the woman who owns the bed and breakfast—said she remembered something about that in Chester Emerson's diaries."

Lester raised an eyebrow. "Instagram photo?" he said.

"Yes, I'm assuming you saw the crow on Instagram?" Megan said. "That's why you're here?"

Lester shook his head. "No, we got a rare bird alert. Someone here sent it." He shrugged.

"Oh," said Megan. Who might have sent it? She supposed Carol must have. Carol was more tech-savvy than Megan gave her credit for. And she and Betty went birding all the time. It would make sense for them to send out an alert.

Megan looked at the man again. "You're a birder?" she said. With all the eagles in the area, birders were not uncommon in Emerson Falls, but usually they came by at a different time of year. Winter. Winter into spring.

"Yes," Lester said. "There was an extremely rare bird out at Puget Sound just the other day. Extremely rare. Many of us were in the area for that. I saw the alert for this crow, and I thought, why not come?" He paused, lost in the memory of his decision. "Why not come?" he repeated after a moment.

The tumble of words, a change from his earlier brevity, made Megan think he might be warming to her. "Have you seen it?" she asked. "The caramel crow?" She looked up at the treetops, but she knew her untrained eyes were unlikely to spot much.

"No," Lester said. "Not yet. Thought I'd get here before the others got here and scared it away. Some birders don't know how to stay quiet. Besides, it's a nice place you have here." He looked at the falls again, cascading down, the clear water frothing itself into white.

"It's one of my favorite spots," Megan said, and then she fell quiet again. Something about this man made her want to simply exist in his presence. She could imagine birds feeling safe enough around him to let themselves be seen. Maybe even alight on his hands and shoulders, like Cinderella's helpers. The thought made her smile.

After a while, she stretched, and her curiosity got the best of her. She couldn't help but ask questions. It's why she loved books so much. They were full of knowledge. "How long have you been birding?" she asked. "What got you started?"

Lester's lips tilted into a smile of reminiscence. He looked down at his hands, but his eyes were looking into the past.

"Many years. Many many years. Well, it would have been the pterodactyl, wouldn't it? When I was a kid. Pterodactyls." He looked up at a spot of sky high over the trees, his gaze being drawn back even farther in time. "Can you imagine seeing one? *Pterodactylus antiquus*, with its wingspan of maybe three feet and change. How wonderful that would have been. *Pteranodon*, however, a pterosaur, had a wingspan of nine to twenty feet. And then there was *Coloborhynchus capito* with its wingspan of twenty-three feet. They didn't discover that one until just a few years ago. If they'd found that while I was a kid ..." His eyes were still in the past, glistening. "They may not have lived here. None of them. Probably not here. But you never know. Of course, pterodactyls weren't actually birds. Or dinosaurs, even. They were flying reptiles. And these birds"—he waved in the direction of the trees, imagining the birds he knew were there, whether they saw them or not—"didn't evolve from pterodactyls. Our modern birds evolved from dinosaurs."

"They did?" Megan said, looking up into the ancient sky Lester saw. "I guess I thought pterodactyls were the first birds. So if they weren't, what was?"

A hearty chuckle came out of Lester. "Well! Isn't that the question. *Archaeopteryx* is the one most people call the first bird, a weak old thing, could probably hardly fly. But a few years back I started hearing word of a new oldest bird. *Aurornis xui*. I never did hear whether they settled that one. I stick to modern birds now. The ones that are alive."

Megan nodded. She, too, preferred to focus on the present more than the past. "Were they the biggest birds ever?" she asked. "The *Colo*... the one with the twenty-three foot wing-span? Or the ... the *Archie* one?"

"*Archaeopteryx* wasn't that big," Lester said, shaking his head. He spread his hands, measuring an invisible bird. "Less than two feet from head to tail. As for the biggest, in our modern world, a good number of albatrosses battle it out for top spot. There's a list, of course, ranking them, but I say they're all with-in a rogue feather, and who's to judge? The royal albatross and wandering albatross have wingspans of nearly twelve feet. Your average room in your average house is eight feet, so add four more feet to that. That's more than two of you stacked on top of each other." He glanced at her, only marginally concerned about whether he'd estimated her height correctly. "Some pelicans come close. The great white, the dalmation. Out this way, your trumpeter swan. They can get to nearly ten feet in wingspan."

"Trumpeter swans can?" said Megan. "I had no idea they were so big."

"Your bald eagles," he said, nodding at the treetops again as though his instincts told him some were perched there, "are nearly six feet, up to maybe seven and a half feet. Think how big those look to your eye. Then imagine three or almost four times that. That's your *Pelagornis sandersi*. That's the biggest, maybe. From twenty-five million years ago. But imagine how majestic that would have been to see it. Incredible. Last I checked, there was only one fossil ever found of *Pelagornis sandersi*. Hard to make a scientific study out of a sample size of one. However, the one they found had a wingspan of twenty to twenty-four feet. When scientists discovered that fossil, they could barely believe it could have flown. Can you imagine? Wouldn't want to be sitting under one of those after it had digested a big meal, I'll tell you that."

Lester spoke so seriously that it took a moment for Megan to realize he'd made a joke. He watched her with those bright eyes, those dark limbal rings, and he saw the moment she made the connection. He smiled.

"So you study dinosaurs—flying reptiles—too?" Megan asked.

He shrugged. "Not really. If something comes across my desk I'll read about it. But mostly it's birds."

His mind, she sensed, was a steel trap of facts about flying creatures.

"What draws you to them?" Megan asked. "What keeps you coming back?"

Lester was quiet for more than a minute, thinking, digging into his heart. Megan was patient, waiting.

"Birds represent our souls," he said at last. "Maya Angelou. The author. Speaker. Her book, *I Know Why The Caged Bird Sings*. She got it. We are meant to be free." He stopped again and thought a while longer. "She said, 'You only are free when you realize you belong no place—you belong every place—no place at all.'" He nodded, the words resonating with him as he spoke them.

"What do you think that means?" Megan asked. "What does it mean to you?"

Lester inhaled, then let out a breath. His eyes seemed always to be scanning the trees, the sky, the landscape; if a mosquito flew by, Megan thought he might see it. Finally, Lester answered. "That quote is from when she was talking to that Bill guy, Bill Moyer, about freedom. Maya knew birds. And she knew souls. And she knew freedom. Look up at that sky," he said, pointing again at the small spot of blue above the trees. "The sky is freedom. All any of us wants is to fly. I suppose that quote could mean a lot of things. I think one thing she meant is that you can never be free if you're not willing to fly."

"But maybe not everyone is meant to fly. I mean, look at penguins," Megan said.

Lester nodded. "Penguins. The ratites—ostriches, emus, kiwis, cassowaries. Domesticated chickens and ducks. Well, those ones can fly, but not for long. But their ancestors could fly. Flightless birds didn't evolve flightless. They started out flying, then lost their ability to fly through evolution. By not flying. Some people think they're penguins when in fact we're all eagles. Eagles, or crows, or songbirds, or falcons, or owls, or you name it. But whatever kind of person, we are all like the birds. We are all meant to fly."

He paused again, and Megan thought he was done talking. She was about to say goodbye and head home when Lester spoke again.

"Not so long ago they found an emperor penguin in Antarctica with almost all black feathers. Normally, of course, they have white breast feathers. The black makes it easier to spot in the snow. Easier prey. Less likely to survive to adulthood," Lester said. "Being different is not necessarily better for survival. But, oh, when they find you, how they stop and stare. I think I'd like to see that one. An old bird, surviving against all odds." He scratched the skin next to his eye. Crow's feet, Megan thought. He had definite, defined crows feet. From squinting into the sun? From laughing?

Lester continued. "This caramel crow, it's beautiful and we're all looking for it, but its coloring is a danger to it. The others won't like it as much. They might not mate with it. It might be shunned. Alone." A sad, serious look fell over his face as he seemed to be going inward for a moment. "In nature," he said when he spoke again, "it's the ones that fit in that survive. Standing out means death. You have to ask, what was it that let the all-black penguin survive?"

"Maybe it was loved more?" said Megan, seeing that there was more to this conversation than birds that didn't belong. "Maybe it was loved so much that the others protected it?"

Lester smirked lightly. "Maybe. Doubtful. That's not how nature works. That's not even how humans work. More likely it was a good bit of luck, and making itself fit in some other way, making itself useful. And probably a lot of determination. Survival instinct is strong, but not always strong enough to keep us oddballs alive."

He looked again to the trees, and for just a moment a sunbeam hit him, scanning across his broad shoulders before the sun's light was covered again by a tree or a cloud.

"You think you're an oddball?" Megan asked gently. "You're an all-black emperor penguin? A caramel crow?"

Lester laughed, crinkling the wrinkles at the edges of his eyes. "I should be so lucky," he said. He turned his neck, seeing past Megan, looking back toward the town. "Then again, maybe I am."

FOUR

Both the beds and the breakfasts at Lily's bed and breakfast were quickly becoming legendary. Lily and her husband Steve had started with an inn with three bedrooms, but then the property next door went up for sale. They'd bought it, renovated it, and connected the space to their original inn to add six more en suite bedrooms and a second gathering room. Lily's attention to detail meant that each bedroom was designed to give her guests the perfect home away from home. This included nothing but the best mattresses, the coziest of blankets, and an abundance of pillows on each bed that guests loved so much they mentioned them in the growing number of reviews. And the breakfasts—adjusted as necessary for any dietary need—filled the guests' bellies, fueling each person for a full day of exploring and sight-seeing, whether that meant hiking, biking, birding, river rafting, winery touring, or any other of the area's favorite activities. Word of mouth was Lily's best advertising.

But despite the perfect king-sized mattress, the soundproofed walls, the impossibly fluffy sheets, and the blackout curtains that kept any light from creeping in, Giles had snored all night long. Candace hadn't fallen asleep until after two, at which point she was dead to the world, and she slept in much later than planned. By the time she and her husband got down to breakfast, Lester was long gone, and most of the other guests had already eaten or were just finishing up their meals.

"Good morning!" Lily greeted them as they sat down at a table. Even after her hours of cooking and serving she was still perfectly coiffed and cheerful. Her shoulder-length auburn hair was pulled back with a wide yellow ribbon at the nape of her neck, and she wore an apron decorated with cherries and cherry pies over her white and yellow polka-dot shirt and yellow capris. "Did you sleep well?"

"Like a baby," Giles said, his eyes drinking in Lily.

Candace swatted his knee. "Well, one of us did."

"You slept!" Giles said. "You're why we're so late!"

"You snored!" Candace started, then she chided herself in her mind. *Act as if.* "I guess I was just so tired after the trip out here, sweetheart. Thank you for waiting for me."

"Where are you from?" Lily asked. Coffee pot in hand, she motioned toward their cups to ask if they wanted any. Candace held up her mug and nodded. Giles declined. Lily carefully poured the hot liquid into Candace's cup.

"Arizona," Candace said. "We are far from home. There was a rare bird out at the coast."

"Very rare," Giles said. "A five."

Lily raised her eyebrows, still smiling. "A five?"

Candace coughed to keep herself from rolling her eyes. "On the rarity scale. A six is extinct. Five is very rare." She smiled at her husband.

"Oh, wow," said Lily. "That must be something! And then our caramel crow out here! Is it that rare too?"

"Caramel crow?" said Giles. "What caramel crow?"

Lily blushed. "Oh, sorry. I was reading the old journals of the gentleman who founded this town. I went back into them when one of our residents mentioned a light-colored crow. That's what he called it. 'Caramel crow' is easier for me to remember than leu … leucitic?"

"Leucistic," said Giles, delighted to be able to show his wisdom to this pretty young thing. "Leucistic. But caramel crow is nice, too. No, I don't think leucistic birds are even on the list. They're mutations, you know. But Candace here wanted to see one, so we came."

"I thought there might also be some owls and eagles that Giles would enjoy," Candace said. "He's retired now and I want him to be happy. Plus, it's about thirty degrees cooler here than it is in Arizona right now. Blazing hot. Unbearable." She fanned her face, as if she could feel the heat that moment.

"Oh, definitely," Lily said. "Perfect weather this time of year here. I should put you in touch with Carol and Betty. They're local birders. They've probably seen every bird we have. Like, literally, every individual bird." She laughed, a golden bell-like laugh that sounded, perhaps, like what angels laughing might sound like.

"That would be lovely," Giles beamed. "You're quite kind."

Just then, Simon came scuffling into the dining area, looking like a man who'd had a rough night. His hair was unwashed and uncombed, like he'd just awakened—which he had. His clothes were the same clothes he'd had on the night before, when he'd met Lily and Megan at Rae's. His eyes looked as red as if he, too, had been kept awake all night by Giles's snoring.

"Good morning, Simon!" Lily said. She turned back to Candace and Giles. "The buffet is open until noon. Cereals, fruit, yogurt, that sort of thing. On the table is a menu of some items I can make from scratch for you if you'd like—pancakes and waffles and egg dishes and such. If you see anything you want, just let me know and I'll get it right out to you." She turned to Simon, who was settling into a seat at a nearby table. "Coffee, Simon?" she said.

"All the coffee," Simon said. "All of it."

Lily laughed and poured. "I'll leave the pot, how's that? You're my last customer for the day."

Simon rubbed his fingers over his eyes. "Perfect. Thank you, Lily."

"Of course. You're so welcome. As I said, let me know if there's anything from the menu on the table that you want. Otherwise, help yourself." She gestured toward the buffet table. "I'll be right back with some cream for those coffees." Lily said, and she whisked herself away to the kitchen.

Candace looked at Simon. He reminded her of her own son. *Her* son, that is, not Giles's. From a mistake she made many years before. Her son, Ronald, had been grown and out of the house before she even started dating Giles. Ronald and Giles had never gotten along so well. Giles had just never understood that Ronald wasn't like him, and that he made different choices. Giles was wealthy and born with a silver spoon in his mouth. Ronald had been lucky to be fed once or twice a day. Candace's early life had not been easy, and she was proud that she'd managed to raise her son, all by herself. So he hadn't become an anesthesiologist. Who really wanted to be an anesthesiologist anyway?

"You here for the leucistic crow?" Candace asked Simon, who was already pouring himself a second cup of coffee.

Simon looked at her like she'd spoken in an alien language. "Sorry?" he said.

"The crow. You're not a birder, then?"

Simon laughed. "No. My car broke down on the highway last night."

"Oh, that's awful," said Giles sympathetically. "Nothing worse than car trouble."

"Well, the kind people of Emerson Falls have taken great care of me," Simon said. He smiled at Lily who was returning with the cream.

"Simon," Lily said, placing a small jar of cream on each table. "I don't know how long you'll need to be here to get your car fixed up, but I checked with my husband. You're a little thinner than he is but I think his clothes might fit you, if you need a change."

"No stores around?" Simon asked.

"Well, not if you don't have a car." Lily laughed again, and the angels sang.

"Then that would be mighty nice of the two of you," Simon said.

"Say, Lily," said Candace. "There was another birder that I think came in last night. Lester. Is he staying here, too?"

"Oh, yes," Lily said. "He was up early, had breakfast at six. We had a nice chat."

"About birds?" asked Giles, slightly jealous of Lester's time alone with Lily.

"Yes, about that crow, and about what else is going on around here," Lily said. "That reminds me, there's a new play in town. We have a brand new theater—literally, they've barely finished painting it. It's in the same building as the library. Quite a space. You really should go look at it if you have time. The dress rehearsal for the first show is tonight, and the opening night is tomorrow."

"Did Lester say he was going to go to the show?" Candace asked, glancing at Giles.

"He was interested in the theater, anyway," Lily said. "But he didn't tell me his plans. I told him where it's located, and told him where Betty and Carol found the caramel crow, and he left shortly after that."

"Hmmm," Candace said. "Young lady, I feel like I should warn you. Lester is a ladies' man. Has been for as long as I've known him. Many a woman has fallen prey to his good looks and his charms." *Myself included*, Candace thought. "Watch out for him."

Lily laughed. "Thank you, but I'm quite happily married. And not interested in looking elsewhere."

Giles looked at his wife and raised an eyebrow in question.

Candace put a placating smile on her face and held his hand.

FIVE

Megan didn't regret the time spent talking with Lester, but her morning walk had taken longer than she'd anticipated. She half-walked, half-jogged back to the library, showered, and got ready for her day, spending some time on plans for a game room she was envisioning in the library downstairs. The main floor was vast, and the space taken up by books couldn't fill the entire floor. There were many rooms and areas yet waiting to discover their purpose. Megan deeply wanted people to come to the library not just for books, but for connection. Loneliness, she knew, was an epidemic around the world. It was her hope to eradicate it in Emerson Falls.

At about eleven-thirty she skipped down the grand staircase that connected the upper level—the living quarters—with the main floor—the library. She headed to a storage room and dug out a couple of power cords, then wove her way through a maze of hallways that created a back passageway to the theater. The public would not generally use this route, but since the theater had once been the garage, the spaces were still connected. An empty hallway at the back of the library ended at a door that led to another empty hallway backstage in the theater. Megan perked her ears to try to hear whether anyone was around, and wound her way forward into the main theater space.

When she got inside the main theater, she couldn't help but take a moment to admire it. She had written, and secured, a grant to help with the funding; community donations had poured in to help. The town was clearly ready for a new source of entertainment. But a good bit of the money used to renovate the space into a theater had been put up by the original owner of the mansion, Edison Finley Wright. He had come to the table with a tremendous vision for the theater—and he was willing to put up the money to make it happen. He had wanted a space that reflected the beauty of the region; something that made people want to attend the theater simply for the experience of being inside a space with such grandeur. In Megan's opinion, the designers, architects, builders, painters, and everyone else involved had exceeded even Edison's hopes and expectations.

The luxurious dark green velvet chairs were set in a gentle curve hugging the stage, reminding Megan of seats around a campfire where everyone was ready to hear a riveting story. Great care had been taken to determine the perfect slope for the auditorium floor so that every member of the audience would have a good view of the stage, and the rows had extra space between them for maximum legroom comfort. The proscenium stage was framed by a soaring arch, onto which a muralist had painted a glorious night sky, with a smattering of stars that continued onto the ceiling above, mimicking the Milky Way. The walls of the theater completed the theme, with paintings depicting the forests and mountains of the North Cascades at night. A few shadowy owls flew through the sky; others perched in trees, ready to watch the show. At the back, a painting of the town's own waterfalls, Emerson Falls, cascaded magnificently down one wall. The aisles between the seats were covered in a deep blue carpet meant to evoke visions of the Skagit River that raced by outside.

The main level held about two hundred seats, and the balcony, another hundred or so. The stage itself was broad, with a rear projection room and projection screen, to help whisk audiences away to other times, ages, worlds. The sound system was state-of-the-art, and even the backstage area had been built to the highest standards, to help attract potential renters. Green rooms and office areas had been fitted out with every possible amenity, and the space below the theater, on the level of the library's downstairs conference rooms, had been converted into a vast area for storage of sets, costumes, and equipment.

The day was still young for the theater company, and the cast and crew were just beginning to congregate to get ready for their dress rehearsal that night. Their energy and excitement were palpable; smiles and hugs and occasional random jumps revealed the adrenaline in each person. Several of the actors were gathered around the director, who was chatting with them casually as more actors arrived. Megan also recognized Tatum, the set director, standing slightly aside from the others, looking out into the audience.

Megan followed her gaze and saw what she was looking at. About halfway back in the seats stood Jace, the theater manager, surveying the scene. Bridget stood by his side, looking mildly annoyed. One hand on her hip, the other carrying a clipboard. She seemed to be waiting for him to say something. Jace seemed unperturbed, or indifferent. He was, Megan, thought, a quirky mix of styles. His blond hair was spiked, and he wore a crisp white button-down shirt, sleeves rolled up, with a bright red-orange bow tie. The frames of his glasses were black and round, reminiscent of Harry Potter. He was tall and lanky, the kind of stature that would make a grandmother sit him down and tell him to eat.

Megan approached the pair, holding the power cords out in front of her. "I brought extras," she said. "Do you still need these?"

"Yes," Bridget said, with a glance at Jace. "Thanks." She took the power cords from Megan and walked off quickly toward the stage. Megan saw that Tatum, still on stage, was now watching Bridget walk with a curious look on her face that Megan couldn't decipher. One eyebrow was slightly raised, and Tatum's top lip was slightly curled on one side. Scorn? Disgust? Or was she just looking at Bridget while she was thinking of something else?

"Busy day," Megan said, turning to Jace. "How's it going?"

"All good," he said, but now he, too, was watching Bridget as she walked away.

Megan didn't know Jace well. He'd been hired to the job from out of town, and had just moved to Emerson Falls a month or two before. If Carol and Betty thought Bridget was a newcomer, what must they think of Jace? Nonetheless, Megan thought he seemed nice enough. Terse, but nice.

"Are you settling into Emerson Falls okay?" Megan asked. "Unpacked and feeling like you're home?"

Finally Jace seemed to realize someone was there talking to him. He turned to Megan and nodded curtly, his mind elsewhere but deciding he had to at least pretend to socialize. "Yes, great, thank you. Nice little town."

"People treating you well?" Megan asked.

Jace laughed. "For the most part."

"Remind me," Megan said, "where were you before this?"

"A small theater in the south end of Seattle," Jace said absently. His eyes returned to Bridget, who was now on stage talking to the director, pointing to the booth at the back of the main floor where the sound and light boards were located. Bridget nodded at the director, and then headed toward the booth.

"What made you move here?" Megan asked.

"Traffic," Jace said, smirking. "The new joke is that Seattle is an hour from Seattle. Here I can walk to work." His attention turned to Tatum, who was still on stage, now watching him with Megan.

"Well, I hope you love it here. We're glad to have you. But I shouldn't keep you. If you need anything else, I'm next door," Megan said, pointing toward the library.

Jace nodded and left, threading his way in the direction of the box office at the front.

Megan made her way back toward the maze of hallways that would take her into the library. As she walked through the dark theater, a beam of light from the back indicated that someone had opened the doors that led into the bright lobby. Megan turned reflexively to see who was there and was surprised to see Lester Heybrook had just walked in, and was now standing at the back of the theater, staring at the stage.

After adjusting to the light for a moment, his eyes scanned the room, looking for something or someone. Unlike most people who walked into the theater for the first time, his attention wasn't drawn by the murals, or the lush seats, or the ribbon of blue carpet he now stood on. Rather, when his eyes found what they were looking for, his attention was fully focused on Bridget, who was standing at the soundboard talking with the sound engineer. Slowly Lester walked over to her. Bridget turned to see who had joined her and the sound engineer, and then Bridget's eyes flew wide open. She looked around, agitated, then said something to Lester and walked away quickly toward the back of the theater, toward the hallways Megan had been heading to herself. Megan tucked herself behind an archway, wanting to watch without being seen. After a few moments, Lester followed Bridget, sauntering more casually, perhaps not to draw attention. Megan held her breath as first Bridget, then Lester, walked past her and into the hallway, but both were absorbed in thought. Neither saw her.

"Well!" Megan whispered under her breath after Lester had gone by. She was sure they were headed to the hallways. Which was where Megan was going; which was where she had been going all along. But now it felt like to follow them would be to intrude. But to intrude on what? Did Bridget know Lester? Or was he harassing her? The latter idea made up Megan's mind. However nice Lester might have seemed when she'd talked with him this morning, Bridget clearly hadn't wanted to see him. And yet he'd followed her. If he was aiming to hurt the young stage manager, Megan wasn't going to let that happen. She straightened her back and headed after them.

Winding her way back through the hallways, Megan thought she'd lost them somewhere in the maze. But when she got to the door between the theater and the library, she paused. Were those voices on the other side of the door? She opened the door slowly, quietly, but her intrusion couldn't go unnoticed. Bridget and Lester paused mid-stream of whatever conversation they might have been having, both looking like highly emotional deer caught in headlights.

Megan stopped and stared at them. "Is everything okay?" she said, looking at Bridget. Her eyes were glistening; her cheeks were bright.

Lester was now looking at the floor, the walls, anywhere but at either Megan or Bridget. Looking guilty. But of what?

"It's all fine," Bridget said. "This gentleman was looking for the bathrooms."

Megan blinked. This was not an entirely implausible explanation; there were bathrooms off the hallway on the theater side of the door. Not public bathrooms, but bathrooms nonetheless. Still, she was certain Bridget was covering for Lester.

Why? She looked from the stage manager to the birder, but both were avoiding her eyes. After a moment, Bridget turned and left abruptly, back through the door to the theater. Lester looked up at Megan, shrugged, and followed Bridget.

Megan's heart clenched. The look on Lester's face had been one of the saddest she'd ever seen.

SIX

At her desk in the library, Megan tried to focus again on the game room for the library, on her general paperwork, on anything outside of the theater, but she couldn't shrug off the vision of despair on Lester's face. What could possibly have transpired between Bridget and Lester in such a short period of time? Did they already know each other? What had they said to each other in those few captured moments in the hallway? Had Bridget asked Lester to follow her to a more private space, or had the older man stalked her?

As she did so often in times of distress, Megan texted Lily.

There's a birder in town, Lester. I think he's staying with you? Megan wrote.

After a few moments, Megan saw three dots indicating Lily was crafting a response. She braced herself for several texts in a row; Lily was what Megan called a "serial texter"—shooting off many short texts rather than one long one.

Yes! came Lily's first text.

Lester Heybrook

Have you met him?

Seems like a nice guy

Quite handsome

Although …

Another guest this morning warned me to watch out for him!!!

Why do you ask?

Megan's brows knitted together.

Someone warned you to watch out for Lester? What did they mean? Watch out in what way? Megan wrote.

Shortly, Lily wrote back:

She didn't say exactly

Woman named Candace Levine.

Husband is Giles

I got the sense he's a womanizer

Lester not Giles

Although I don't know about Giles

I mean he's not hard on the eyes!

Lester not Giles

Have you seen those eyes???

She also told me the other birders call him The Crow

???

Apparently some of them name each other for birds or something?

She said he's annoying

Thus The Crow

Her explanation anyway.

Megan thought back to her conversation with Lester at Emerson Falls. Their talk about the caramel crow, and about how its differences would make it an outsider, not accepted by the "normal" crows. She very much wanted to like Lester. She'd felt an affinity with him. He'd been talking about the birds, the leucistic animals, but the way he spoke of their oddities, she knew being an outsider was something with which he was familiar. She'd wondered then, and wondered again now: does everyone feel like an outsider in some way? Does anyone actually go around feeling like they belong? If only she had the ability to read everyone's minds.

Well, she thought, that's what books are for. That's like mind reading.

She tapped out a reply to Lily.

Yes, those eyes are mesmerizing. He didn't try to womanize me. Did he try anything with you? Do you know anything more about him? Try to find out what you can.

Lily quickly replied:

Will do, boss

But why?

Has he done something?

Megan replied:

Not that I know of. He just keeps showing up everywhere I go, and I'm curious. Plus he has those eyes. Can't help be curious about a guy with nice limbal rings.

Lily wrote back:

Limbal rings??

Will google

Maybe he is trying to womanize you!

I mean, Megan, he could be a catch!

Give him a chance!

Megan could almost hear Lily's sparkling laugh come through in her words.

You are ridiculous. Stop being silly. Text me if you unearth anything.

Lily replied:

Yes, Sherlock!

I'm on the case!

Megan shook her head, smiling as she clicked off her phone. Back to work, she told herself.

She'd been at her desk for another half hour or so when a woman she didn't recognize approached. An older man trailed a few steps behind her, admiring the lofty space of the library and looking distinctly like he was just along for the ride. The woman had long, dry bleached-blonde hair, but looked like she'd aged more than she realized she had. Like she still thought of herself as a twenty-something, when in fact she was more likely about twice that. Her eyes were framed by too much eyeliner, which was bleeding slightly across her lower lids, and her wrinkles indicated a good amount of time spent outside. The older man looked gentler, somehow, but also less curious. Like the world he inhabited and the world of people might not overlap all that often.

"Hi," said Megan cheerfully. "Can I help you?"

"Yes, well, maybe," said the woman. "We came to see the leucistic crow. The bed and breakfast lady told us someone saw it at the falls, but we went there and didn't see it. Do you know if it's been spotted elsewhere?"

"Oh, you're one of the birders!" Megan said, wondering if this was the very Candace and Giles Lily had mentioned. "Well, unfortunately I haven't seen the crow myself; I've just heard some locals talking about it. I know they were down at Emerson Falls when they saw it. You undoubtedly know more than I do about the habits of crows. They stay in the same area for a while at least, don't they?"

"Generally," said the woman. "It's okay. There are plenty other birds around that we can get a gander at. Do you know if there are any books or local guides?"

Megan tapped at her keyboard and brought up a few suggestions. She wrote down the Dewey decimal numbers for the woman, then pointed her to a rack at the front of the library, which held dozens of different brochures on regional activities. "I'm fairly sure there are some pamphlets there that might point you in the right direction," she said.

The woman thanked Megan and turned to leave, but then turned back. "We are here for a few days. Is there anything else that you recommend? What sorts of things have you been pointing other people to lately?"

The way the woman worded her question seemed so awkward, like she wanted to know something more, something specific, something other than just what she was asking. Megan felt like she was being quizzed, but she didn't know the right answer. "Well, there's river rafting, people love that. There are a few dams with some great viewpoints if you drive east out Highway 20 a ways, and lots of hiking pretty much all over. You'd definite-ly have a good chance of seeing some birds out that way. Owls, eagles, birds of prey. Oh, and we have a play tomorrow night, our first play in our new theater." She nodded her head in the direction of the new building. "Dress rehearsal is tonight, and tomorrow there's a party after the first show, downstairs here in the library. Everyone's welcome."

"That sounds lovely," said the woman. Her smile seemed so forced, like it almost hurt her. The man behind her continued to ignore her, his attention instead focused on the high roof, the floor-to-ceiling windows, the reading nook at the center of the room, facing out toward the water. Megan wondered about their relationship. Was it worth it? If they were, in fact, mar-ried, was it worth it to be married to someone who so clearly wasn't interested in what you were doing? On the other hand, she thought, that wasn't fair. He was there, with this woman, and that had to count for something. It did not do, she knew, to make too many assumptions about other people's lives.

"Maybe we'll see you there," Megan said, trying to make her own smile seem more natural. But the woman had already dis-missed her, and was heading out the door, unconcerned with whether the man was following behind.

SEVEN

Friday morning, Megan was up early. The dress rehearsal had gone well the night before, she'd heard, and now today was The Big Day. Everyone in town—everyone she knew, anyway, which was just about everyone—was going to be at the show, as well as the party afterward, to celebrate a new phase in the town's history and growth.

"Possibly, literally everyone," Megan said to her reflection in her mirror as she put on her makeup. "Good night for a burglary, if any burglars are listening." She patted down a stray strand of her long, slightly wavy, dark brunette hair, checking for grays. "Stay away, gray," she said, plucking a silvery-white hair from her temple.

Megan thought she could feel the town vibrating with excitement; or maybe that was just her. Edison Finley Wright had pulled out all the stops for the party tonight, paying for the whole thing himself, which meant that even the most reclusive and introverted people in the town would make an appearance just to experience the pomp. Megan wanted the library to look its best. She and Owen, her employee in charge of the conference space, were planning to take turns watching over the library so that it could also be open during the party. Megan's hope was that party-goers would head upstairs to wander through the stacks, see the list she'd put together on a large poster of all the programs the library offered, and decide to get involved. Some people thought libraries were just about books, but people who used libraries knew they were so much more. Her library was small, and funds were short, but in addition to the book group and the upcoming games room, Megan had already set up a popular computer and internet access area, complete with printers; created an after-school volunteer tutoring program; and put out feelers about a monthly lecture series. The more people saw what was going on, she hoped, the more people might donate, thus enabling her to create more programs, thus inspiring more people to donate, in an endless circle of literary, inspirational, and educational growth.

At about nine-thirty, Megan skipped down the grand staircase to the main level. The library wouldn't be open until noon, but there was much to be done both in the library and the lower level, where she was sure Owen would soon be at work, if he wasn't already. Megan started by pulling out her dusting cloth and vacuum cleaner, and for an hour she swept through every library space, tidying and cleaning and making everything sparkle. With the enormous windows, a sunny day like today made any dust all the more visible. A volunteer came in twice a month to help clean, but Megan wasn't leaving anything to chance.

After that, she propped up the posters and set out the brochures she'd created, detailing the various library programs. Next to these items, she fanned out a stack of donation envelopes she'd had printed up earlier in the week. "You never know who might toss us a few dollars," she said to the envelopes as she adjusted their points into a perfect half-circle.

At eleven, Megan gave her library a satisfied nod. If there was more she could do, she couldn't think of it. She headed downstairs to see how Owen and his crew were managing with party preparations.

Whereas things on the main level had been quiet—just Megan and the songs she'd half-sung, half-hummed as she'd cleaned—down in the conference rooms the energy and feeling of anticipation were electric. In addition to Owen and a few other library staff, half a dozen theater volunteers were helping out. Later, they would take tickets, staff the concessions booth, and guide people to their seats, but for now they were busy laying out tablecloths on the tall bistro tables that had been delivered by the party rental company, putting together floral centerpieces, hanging bright white twinkle lights and festive garlands, and in general creating a party atmosphere that made Megan want to dance.

When Megan saw Owen, a smile lit up her face automatically. His thick, unruly hair would do nothing but stand on end, and Megan always thought he looked like the Heat Miser. His hair was eminently ruffle-able, and Megan imagined anyone dating him would have their hands in his hair all the time. His hair was irresistible. Well, his hair and the fact that he was probably the most competent, even-keeled, intelligent, helpful employee on the planet.

"Owen!" Megan called out as she approached him. The room had a small, low stage, and Owen was busy setting up cables and cords and speakers and microphones for the live band that would be arriving later that evening. "Where's the music?"

Owen looked up and grinned widely. "That, my friend, is a really good idea. Do you have a boom box?" He winked.

Megan laughed. "Boom box! Do they still make those?"

With a chuckle, Owen turned to a laptop by the edge of the stage and loaded Spotify. He found an 80s dance music playlist, then plugged the computer into the speakers. Instantly the room was filled with sound.

"Safety Dance!" Megan said. "I haven't heard this in years!" Some of the volunteers stopped what they were doing to dance to the music, twirling and posing and laughing for a few minutes before getting back to their tasks.

"How's it going upstairs?" Owen asked, turning back to the snakes of cables and cords that seemed completely daunting to Megan.

"Great. All done. What can I do to help here?" Megan said.

Owen nodded his head toward the door that led to a loading dock outside. "Someone came by with a bunch of flowers for the theater, and for some reason left them here. Want to take those upstairs to the theater folks?"

"Happy to do it," Megan said. "And then have another job ready for me when I get back; the library doesn't open until twelve and I've got nothing but time!" She headed to the loading dock door, which was propped open to let in the fresh air. Just outside were two large bouquets, bright white cards poking out of their centers. Megan read the names and recognized them as the two leads, the actors playing Maria and the Captain. "Aw, that's nice," Megan said to the flowers.

From the conference center's loading dock where she stood, the quickest route to the theater was around to one of the back entrances to the theater. Megan lifted the heavy flowers, balancing one on each hip, and inhaled the fresh floral scents as she walked the short path. When she got to the door, it was locked. She put the flowers down, tapped the code into the keypad, and headed inside.

Loud voices floated to her from somewhere within the nearby rooms. Megan thought she recognized Bridget's voice as one of them. The other voice was lower, a man's rumbling voice, though Megan couldn't determine whose it was. Lester again?

Was he back harassing Bridget?

"It's not fair!" Megan heard Bridget yell just as she turned the corner into the room where she saw Bridget arguing with Jace.

Bridget's pale face was covered in tears; a few strands of her dark, blunt-cut hair were stuck to her cheeks. Jace stood looking at her, hands on his hips, his face a mixture of calm and frustration. Like they'd been having this conversation for a while and he didn't know what else to say. On Megan's interruption, both looked up. Bridget wiped her face and turned to the wall, hugging herself with her arms.

"Yes?" Jace said, his tone indicating that this had better be a short visit.

"Oh, sorry, I—" Megan said, watching Bridget's body language for signs of fear or danger. Seeing none, she sighed. "Someone delivered these to the conference rooms," she said. "They're for your actors. Just thought I'd bring them by."

Jace took the flowers from Megan and set them on the floor. "Thank you," he said. "Anything else?"

Megan looked at Bridget. Did she need help? It was none of her business. No one seemed unsafe here. "No, that's it. Let me know if you guys need anything," she said, trying to will her words into Bridget's ears, trying to make sure their intended meaning was understood.

"Will do," Jace said. His hands returned to his hips and he turned slightly, creating a barrier between Megan and the rest of the room. A not-so-subtle message that it was time for her to go.

Megan took her time walking back to the conference rooms, outside under the sun. How would a person know when to step in? Any number of conversations might look suspicious from the outside. Was she getting too caught up in the idea of herself as a detective? Even though Max, the local Deputy, had told her she was part of his team and given her a toy police badge to prove it, that was just words. Was she putting her nose where it didn't belong?

"Probably," Megan said to the crisp blue sky as she watched an eagle float effortlessly on the wind. She headed back in to see what Owen needed next.

EIGHT

Whether the opening night performance merited the two standing ovations it received would be a matter of general town discussion, but the audience was generous and effervescent in its enthusiasm. Family members and friends and town residents and visitors alike were swept up in the energy of the evening, and they took that energy in full force with them downstairs to the afterparty. An hour past the end of the show, the music was blaring, people were dancing, drinks were flowing. Megan couldn't see it from her post upstairs in the library, but she could imagine the cheer spread across the tired but happy faces of actors and audience alike.

Lily, far more of a morning person than a night person, looked about ready to fall asleep when she found Megan in the library.

"You're still here!" Lily said, blinking hard, as if an extra long blink could count as a nap and refresh her.

"Oh honey," Megan said, laughing. "Are you heading home? I need to find you some toothpicks for your eyes!"

"Yes, Steve's outside waiting for me. I may have to have him

carry me! I'm so tired I feel drunk." Lily rubbed her eyes carefully so as not to disturb her makeup.

"Everything going well downstairs?" Megan asked. "Not a
ton of people have come up here. A couple of people picked up
donations envelopes, but that's about it. I think it was a good
idea, but I'm ready to close up." Though the walls were thick
and generally didn't carry much sound, Megan could sense the
music more than she could hear it. The tiniest vibration, a deep
thumping in the floor.

"It's still going strong," Lily said. "You should definitely close
up and head on down." She yawned widely, covering her mouth
with a delicate hand.

"You go on home," Megan said. "Call me tomorrow."

Megan walked Lily to the front door and locked it up behind
her, then went through the library, closing up, turning off lights,
shutting off the copier, the computers, and the printers. She
locked the last door behind herself and headed downstairs.

The wave of music that greeted her was almost physical. Megan was glad the library had no close neighbors to complain.
The only person who lived within any short distance was herself, up on the top floor. The sound would be pouring out the
open sliding glass doors in the convention area, and drifting up
to her own rooms. If she was going to be kept awake by it anyway, she thought, she may as well dance.

When she got to the conference rooms, the walls of which
had all been opened up to create the biggest space possible, she
felt a surge of joy on seeing just about everyone she knew. Even
Rae was there, having closed down the pub early for the night.
Megan caught her eye and waved.

On just a quick glance, Megan saw several of the actors from
the show, as well as many people from behind the scenes. And
the out-of-towners had made their way to the party as well. Lester was there, standing off to the side, a beer in his hand, a small

smile on his face. The couple who had come to the library earlier were there, Candace and Giles. Giles still looked like he'd just been told to come; Candace was talking to a man with dark hair and a black leather jacket, who Megan didn't recognize. Another birder, maybe? Carol and Betty were standing at a table, and Carol's hips were moving like she'd been boogying all night and was just taking a break.

On the dance floor, Megan was delighted to find Officer Max Coleman, the Deputy whose beat included Emerson Falls, busting some moves and singing along at the top of his lungs to "Jessie's Girl."

"Max!" Megan said, dancing up alongside the Deputy, one of her favorite people. "I have never seen you quite so loose! Have you been drinking?"

The color in Max's face rose and he smiled his perfect dimpled smile, the lights from the mirror balls glistening off his unblemished teeth. "Megan!" he said. "No, just letting off some steam. Haven't seen you for a while! How are you?"

"I'm good!" Megan yelled. "How are you?" She moved effortlessly into her version of The Sprinkler dance. The look on Max's face was priceless. Whether he was laughing with or at her, she didn't care.

"What?" Max yelled back. "I can't hear you!"

"Sorry, I can't hear you," Megan said, showing off what some might have vaguely recognized as The Running Man move.

Max shook his head and joined in.

When the song ended, Max gently led Megan to the side of the dance floor. Megan put her hands over her ears to try to stop the ringing. "Has it been this loud all night?" she asked, and the music began again.

Max pointed to the sliding glass doors that led outside, and Megan nodded.

Outside, the stars were shining bright over the river. Even

just a few feet from the doors, the still of the night reached out, beckoning them further into the peace. They headed down to the river, leaving the pulsing music behind, replaced by the everlasting shushing of the water.

"Looks like everyone is having a good time," Megan said as they sat at a cluster of benches by the river. "I'm so pleased. This is what I was hoping for from this place. It's perfect."

"You've done well," Max said gently, the moonlight reflecting in his eyes.

"Ah, you're too kind," Megan said. "None of it was me. But thanks anyway."

"Well, some of it was you," Max said. "I know you. You matter in this town, Megan. I hope you know that."

Megan felt herself blush in the darkness.

For a while, they watched the moonbeams dance on the ripples of the river, listening to the sounds of the night, feeling the cool September air as it dried the dance sweat from their bodies. Megan shivered.

"Getting cold?" said Max. He took off his jacket and put it around Megan's shoulders. She realized she rarely saw him out of uniform. Not that he didn't look good in a uniform; he was a fairy tale prince, and looked good in anything. But for the show tonight, he'd donned a well-fitting dark navy jacket over a slightly off-white collarless shirt, with trousers to match the jacket. He looked good.

Megan welcomed the warmth of the gesture as well as the jacket. She was, indeed, getting cold, but she didn't want to go in just yet. The music inside seemed distant; the magic of the night was lingering outside, there, under the stars.

After a few minutes, however, another sound broke the spell. At first, the blare of sirens made Max and Megan look at each other in puzzlement. The wailing alert, cutting through the night air and getting closer, wasn't coming from Max's police car, obviously. What was it? Next thing they knew, the echoes of emergency lights were lighting up the tops of the trees around them. The vehicle seemed to pull into the lot on the other side of the library and stop. The sound cut out ominously.

Max and Megan ran inside, where the music had stopped and people were milling in chaos. "What's happening?" Megan said to whoever would listen.

Whatever had happened, it hadn't happened in the conference room. The sounds of people talking and crying out all over the building confused the issue further. Megan turned to Max. "The theater?" she suggested. Megan and Max raced through a maze of rooms until they came to the theater storage rooms, but saw no one there. They ran upstairs and through the hallways, ears perked to pick up any sounds. Finally, just as they reached the theater, they saw someone being wheeled out on a gurney, up the dark blue carpets that mimicked the Skagit River, and out to the ambulance waiting outside.

Megan looked around to see who was there, who could tell her anything. Jace was talking to emergency personnel. After a few moments he ran out of the theater, following the gurney. Tatum stood on stage, pale.

"Tatum!" Megan said, running up the stairs to the stage, Max close behind. "What happened?"

Tatum looked like she was in shock, breathing shallowly, shivering. "She threw up, then fainted," she said.

"Who?" said Megan. "Who, Tatum?"

"Bridget."

The mood in the conference rooms, previously so jovial, was somber as everyone awaited news. Some had gone home, but many were waiting to hear word that Bridget would be okay.

Max was first to get the notice. A call from the hospital. All eyes were on him as he held his phone to his ear.

The look on his face told the group everything they needed to know.

He hung up the phone and shook his head.

People slowly filtered out of the room almost noiselessly, taking in the news of Bridget's death. Whispered gasps of "I can't believe it" and "she was so young" followed people out the door. When only a few people were left, Megan noticed Lester had stayed behind. He was looking at her intently, seemingly struggling with a conversation in his mind.

Finally, he approached.

"It was Bridget who died," he said, his voice wavering.

"Yes," said Megan. Why did this man care?

"You're the police," Lester said, looking at Max.

"I am," Max said.

Lester paused and took a jagged breath.

"You're going to need her real name," Lester said. He looked pale and shell-shocked. "To investigate."

"Her real name?" said Megan. "It's not Bridget Hill?"

Lester shook his head slowly. "No. No. She was … she was in the witness protection program. Her name is … was … Branwen. Branwen Heybrook. She was my daughter."

NINE

I held Joel's free hand and we sat there saying nothing. He turned to watch the tattoo artist as she finished up. All three of us, eyes riveted to his arm. The quiet was as thick as a down jacket on a hot day; the only sound was the buzz of the tattoo machine.

A tattoo pen, I thought, writing my future.

When Joel was done, the tattoo artist cleaned up and then set me into the chair.

"I'll hold your hand," Joel said, sitting in the seat I'd warmed. "What are you getting?"

"A tiny raven in white ink," I said, pulling a paper out of my shorts pocket. I unfolded it to show him the drawing I'd chosen to have permanently inked onto my skin, then gave it to the artist. I pointed to my right ankle. "Here."

"Why not…" he said, then paused. He reached toward my chest and lightly, like a feather, touched the skin at the top of my left breast. "…here?" He touched me only for a second, a millisecond, but his fingers blazed fire through my body. "On your heart?"

I had to remind myself to breathe.

Forty minutes later, we were eating ice cream by the lake. He reached out, held his fingers just millimeters above my chest. The bandage still covered the tattoo but I could feel his heat radiating from his hand.

"So I should know your name," he said, looking at the bandage like he could see through it, straight to my heart.

"Branwen," I said. "Bran."

"Branwen, huh?" he said. He lifted his eyes past me, squinted into the hot sun. "That a family name?"

"Sort of," I said. "I'm sort of named after my father."

"Sort of?" he said, turning his eyes from the sun to me.

"It means 'fair raven,'" I said. "Or technically, 'raven fair.' Bran is raven. Gwen is fair."

He smiled, putting the pieces together, looked at my chest, through the bandage again. "Fair raven. That's why the white ink?"

"That's why the white ink."

"I'm Joel," he said. "Just Joel. It means Joel." He smiled broadly, pleased with himself.

"Nice to meet you, Joel."

TEN

Max called in the forensics team while Megan sat with Lester, not knowing quite what to say. Once Max had the team up to speed and running, he returned to the somber scene in the conference rooms.

He shook his head. "The U.S. Marshals are the ones who run the witness protection program. I called them to let them know one of their people had been killed. They were not, shall I say, particularly open to giving out information. Tight ship they run there. The guy I talked to said they'll inform the FBI, but in the meantime, there's not much they can do, now that she's gone."

"I've heard that they're pretty secretive," Megan said. "We have a book about them in the library. Something like *WITSEC: Inside the Witness Protection Program*, I think. I can't remember what WITSEC stands for?" She looked at Lester, but he merely shrugged.

"Lester," Max said. "Are you in the program, too? Are you in danger?" He pulled a folding chair next to Megan's and sat down, leaning forward, elbows on knees, his face earnest.

"Oh, no," said Lester. "No, not me." He stared at the tall windows and scratched the corner of his eye. They had closed the doors against the night chill, so with the bright lights inside all he could see was the reflection of himself, the reflection of Megan and Max. He watched himself, seeming to study himself in his grief. *This is what grief looks like. This is what I look like on the day my daughter dies.*

"How did you know she was here, then?" Max asked. "Did she tell you? Were you in communication? Or was it coincidence? How did you find her?"

Lester pulled his eyes away from his reflection and looked at his hands. He sighed and started his story much further back. "I did not raise Branwen," he said. "I was not there. I was there for a short time, when she was young." A sad smile tilted the corner of his lips. "We were best buddies then. For a few years. But I wasn't made to be tied down." He looked at Megan. "I thought I was meant to fly." He studied the lines on the back of his hands for a long while, the creases of time and age, of wind and sun, of a past that could not be changed. "Maybe I was wrong." He paused again, longer. Max and Megan were silent, letting Lester continue on his own time.

After a few minutes, Lester spoke again. "Her mother is dead and I didn't keep in touch with Bran like I should have. I didn't know she'd met up with a guy. I didn't know there was trouble. First thing I knew of it—" he looked up at the lights on the ceiling, like there were secrets there—"first thing I knew, I got a letter from her. Through the marshals. She gave it to them, they opened it and read it, then they sent it on to me. She explained a bit of what happened. That she'd gone into the program. That she couldn't tell me her name, or where she was. That she…" His voice wavered and caught. He breathed out a puff of air, hard, trying to recompose himself. "That she loved me, and hoped to see me again one day." Tears filled his eyes, a flash flood out of nowhere, and started to stream down his cheeks.

Megan put a hand on his arm. Lester covered it with his own hand.

"She signed it 'your fair raven,'" Lester said. "That's what her name means. Branwen. Fair raven. The other birders started calling me The Crow before she was even born. She was named for me." Silently, he started to weep.

Max paused, wanting to be considerate of Lester's pain but also needing to gather information. After a few minutes, he pressed on. "So how did you know she was here?" he asked.

"The rare bird alert," Lester said, shaking his head. He laughed. "Strange. I normally wouldn't have paid any attention to a leucistic bird. Not gone out of my way for it, anyway. The alert was sent by someone whose user name was Fair Raven. I saw it and I got a chill. Could that have been her? I just had ... I just had this feeling. Couldn't explain it. Just a feeling. I had to find out. I had to come, just to see."

Megan could imagine the draw. To have lost your child to the witness protection program, never knowing if you'd see her again, and then here was a light, a beacon. You'd have to go. She would have done the same.

"But why do you think she risked it?" Megan asked, already knowing the answer.

"I didn't have much chance to talk to her," Lester said, his eyes sliding toward Megan without actually looking at her. "So I can mostly only guess. She missed family. She missed being around people she knew. She couldn't talk to anyone. Couldn't open up to anyone. Had to hold everything in. She couldn't be herself." He shrugged. "She just wanted a moment, I suppose, with someone who she knew would love her forever. Someone she could trust. Even if I wasn't always there, she always knew I loved her." A sudden sob burst out of him. "I hope."

Megan's face flushed with shame of having broken Lester and

Bridget apart, up in the hallways between the library and the theater. If only she'd left them alone! They could have had a few more minutes together. Minutes that could now never be replaced. Yes, she'd been trying to help Bridget … Branwen … No, to Megan, she was Bridget. Regardless of the woman's name, it turned out Megan had stolen some of her last moments with her father. Megan felt a tornado of regret inside her, of wanting to turn back time and leave father and daughter alone. Give them time and space to talk, to heal, to mend. But it was too late.

Max looked at Megan, perhaps seeing what was going through her head. He turned to Lester. "It's late. I'll want to talk with you more in the morning, but for now, why don't you go back to the B&B." He pulled out a business card. "Call me if you need anything," he said.

Megan nodded. "Or me. Anything."

Lester stood, a process that looked more like a painful unraveling of his body. He seemed to have aged ten years in the past hour. "All right," he said. "I will see you tomorrow, I suppose."

"Do you need a ride?" Megan asked. "I can drive, if you like."

Lester shook his head sadly. "The only thing I need is to have my daughter back."

By the time Megan made it to bed, it was very late. It was a strange feeling, knowing that the forensics team was downstairs, working meticulously to find anything that could help them figure out who had killed Lester's fair raven. Megan couldn't imagine the DNA would be much help. Nearly everyone in town had been at the show. All the visitors. People from all the neighboring towns. Everyone's DNA would be everywhere. Megan remembered Tatum saying that Bridget had thrown up before she fainted. Undoubtedly the forensics team would be looking for whatever cup she might have taken a drink from, but there would be hundreds of cups to look at. The task ahead seemed nearly impossible.

As Megan fell asleep, she hoped desperately the night would bring no dreams.

ELEVEN

Megan's brain worked on theories and questions all night. She awoke exhausted but determined.

She dived into detective mode before even getting herself a coffee. Her laptop was sitting on her bedside table, and she sat up and pulled it onto her lap in bed. Once the screen had finished loading, she started searching.

Which poisons kill quickly, she typed into the search bar. She knew the search was pointless; the forensics team would determine exactly what the cause of death was. But she felt the need to do something. And, she was curious.

"Don't worry, FBI, I'm not planning anything," Megan said to the room, looking around vaguely, knowing they wouldn't descend on her for this online search ... or would they? No. Definitely not.

The long list of articles that flowed onto Megan's screen let her know she was far from the only person interested in the topic. She couldn't decide if this was reassuring or disturbing. What was the appeal, anyway? Was it preventative? After all, knowing what would kill meant knowing what to avoid. Like tetrodo-toxin, the toxin in pufferfish that people, mostly in Japan, ate knowingly and willingly, a thrilling game of Russian roulette with food. The pufferfish, if prepared correctly, was a delicacy. If prepared incorrectly, it would kill. The toxin was heat stable, so cooking made no difference; the parts of the fish containing the toxin must be cut away with expert precision. Symptoms from a fatal dose, she read, would begin in barely more than a quarter of an hour of ingestion.

The event last night had been catered, but Megan severely doubted any pufferfish had been on the table. She set tetrodo-toxin aside in her head in the "possible but highly unlikely" category.

She continued reading through the list. Arsenic, the old standby made famous by murder mystery writers. And, Megan learned, once the poison of choice for women wanting to get rid of their husbands, due to how easy it once was to buy. Vomiting, seizures, and death, all within a few hours, in high doses, but these days it was not so easy to procure. An article about "how to get arsenic out of your rice" caught Megan's eye, but that seemed like such a grueling process that she put arsenic aside, as well.

Megan made her way through many lists. Botulinum was powerful when ingested in the right doses. Kills the nervous system, causes extreme pain. Ricin could be ingested or inhaled; death would occur within hours. Anthrax, of course, was most commonly inhaled, leading to a collapse of the respiratory system. Sarin was hundreds of times more toxic than cyanide, which itself would lead to death within minutes. Amatoxin. Mercury. Strychnine. Compound 1080. Digoxin, polonium, atropine, VX, batrachotoxin, maitotoxin, thallium.

A few of them created by humans, most of them naturally occurring—but extracted by humans for deadly purposes. Or, in the case of one of the most toxic substances known to mankind, willingly injected into foreheads to create the appearance of youth. Such a toxic world, Megan thought. How did humans make it this far? How did anyone make it through alive?

Of course, she thought, no one made it through alive. Death was a part of the deal. You're born, you do your best to live through all the fears and challenges and heartaches and impossible, unbearable pain, and you die.

Or, in a few unlucky cases, someone kills you.

"Well, you are a ray of sunshine this morning, Megan Montaigne," Megan said. She shut down her laptop and got ready for the day.

While Megan was finally relaxing on her balcony with a second cup of much-needed coffee, her phone buzzed with an incoming text. Max.

Her heart skipped a beat. Had they discovered something? Had they uncovered the cause of death so quickly?

She read the text.

You're a librarian. You like to read.

Megan laughed out loud. Here she'd been expecting to see something about ricin or digoxin. She shook her head.

You are astute. Is that why you're a police officer? she wrote.

I am not just astute, Max wrote. *I am two-stutes. Get it? A stute, two stutes?*

Megan chuckled and groaned at the same time.

Someone is bright and cheeky this morning, she wrote.

Every day I'm alive is a good day, Max said.

Megan's mood sobered. Yes, she thought. Every day I am alive is a good day. From now on, every day I'm alive, I'm a day luckier than Bridget Hill. Than Branwen Heybrook.

You're not wrong there. Yes, I like to read, she wrote back. *What's up?*

I've been going through Bridget's house, Max wrote. *She kept journals. Stacks of them. We're short staffed. Soooooo …?*

Yes! Megan wrote. *I can read them. Find clues. Take notes.*

It would be a big help, Max wrote. *Confidential of course. I've cleared it with the boss. We're considering you a consultant.*

Yes, Chief! I'm your woman. I'm your reader.

Deputy. Not Chief.

Chief to me.

You're the best. I'll bring them by in half an hour? Max wrote.

I'll be ready.

Megan sighed with satisfaction and smiled at the river. Permission to read someone else's journals. If she was honest, it felt almost as wrong as poisoning someone. Not really, of course, but journals were not meant for anyone but the person who wrote them. Journals were a secret cave, a hidden vault where people stored the things that were too heavy to hold in their minds. The journals of a person in the witness protection program … well. The idea of reading the journals felt wrong, but also Megan was almost giddy with the thrill of diving into someone else's mysterious inner world. "We are going to figure this out," she said to the river. "Secrets are never buried forever."

Megan turned her face to the sun and soaked in the life it brought, imagining tiny workers in her cells turning the UVB rays into vitamin D. It never ceased to amaze her that humans still had this in common with plants: the need to get at least some nourishment from that closest star. *Photolysis*. The word popped into her mind. She'd heard the word but couldn't remember the process. But it didn't matter. Her body knew what to do with the sun. All she needed to do was give it the chance.

Shortly, her phone buzzed again, this time with a notification that someone was at the door downstairs. Checking the camera to make sure it was Max, she tapped the app and let him in.

"Coffee?" Megan said as she opened the door to the handsome police officer. His dark, slightly wavy hair was never tidy but also never messy; it always just existed in a state of casual perfection. He was a stunning figure in or out of his uniform, Megan thought, and then almost laughed out loud at her unintended mental euphemism.

"You're happy," Max said, bringing out his dimples and his teeth so white they lit up the room. He lifted a paper bag he was carrying. "Journals."

"Always happy to see you, Chief," Megan said. She took the journals from Max and put them down for the time being, then headed to the kitchen. Max followed. Soon she had two fresh mugs of coffee ready.

"Balcony?" she said.

"Always time for the balcony," Max said.

The day was beautiful, but the morning was still slightly chilly. Megan grabbed an extra blanket for Max—hers was already outside—and led him out onto the balcony.

"So nice out here," Max said. He took a deep breath in and turned his face to the sun.

Megan smiled. Humans are like sunflowers, she thought. When we're not caught up inside our heads, that is. Humans will turn to the sun.

"I love it out here," said Megan. "I can never get enough of the water. It's my element." She paused and looked at the sky, imagined people who spent their days looking to the sky. "I suppose Lester's element would be air. What are you?"

Max guffawed. That was one of the things Megan liked about him. When he laughed, he meant it. No fake laughs, no pity laughs. Guffaws and chuckles and those dazzling smiles. When Officer Max laughed, the world laughed with him.

"I have not the slightest idea. What are my options?" he said. "Water, air, … dirt?"

"Close," Megan said. "Water, air, earth, fire." She studied him a moment. "There's no question, really. You're earth. Solid. Grounded. Steady."

"And you're water?" Max said. Megan nodded. "Why water?" Max asked.

She shrugged. "Why do you think?"

Max tilted his head, thinking. He looked out at the river for inspiration, then back at Megan. "You run deep. Is that too cliché?"

"Not at all," Megan said. "What else?"

Max looked at the water again. "You persevere," he said after a few moments. "Given enough time, nothing can stop you." He smiled. "Close?"

Megan beamed. "That's good. You've paid for your coffee with that."

Max chuckled again and took a sip from his mug.

"So what do they have?" Megan said. "Anything yet?"

"Not much," Max said, shaking his head. "The samples have gone to the lab."

"Let me know what they find out?" Megan asked.

Max nodded. "I'm meeting Lester at ten. If you're looking for something to do—"

Megan nodded vigorously. She was always interested.

"—you should talk to that couple, the other birders. And Lester. Anyone in town who's not normally in town. I'll be talking to everyone too, but people often hold back when talking to the police. They're afraid every gumball they ever stole will come back to haunt them. Don't make any accusations or anything, obviously. But maybe you can suss out some information."

"Suss. Done. Check. I'm on it," Megan said. The library was closed for the weekend. She could put everything into this effort.

"An FBI guy is on his way in," Max said, almost offhandedly.

"Oh?" said Megan. This wasn't a complete surprise. She wasn't sure what the protocol would be for a death of someone in the witness protection program, but she figured someone official would make an appearance sooner or later.

"Should be here later today or tomorrow," Max said. He set his mug on the table beside him and shook his head. "Something is off about this …"

Megan waited, but Max didn't continue.

"Something is off?" she pressed.

He shook his head. "I just don't know. Keep your eyes and ears open, that's all I can say. If you learn anything …"

"You will be the first person I call," Megan said.

"And with that," Max said, swallowing down the last gulp of coffee, "I have to get back to work." He stood. "Don't write in those journals, but do take notes. Anything that seems weird or telling or could lead somewhere. Anything you think needs another mind working on it. Anything that could help. And thank you."

TWELVE

Lily placed a platter with a mountain of blueberry pancakes and a bowl of perfectly scrambled eggs with diced ham and melted cheese onto Candace and Giles's table. "The blueberries are from our garden," she said. "Fresh as can be. If you need anything else, let me know." She turned to clear a table that other guests had just left.

While Giles dug into the pancakes, serving himself a stack of three, Candace spooned a heap of eggs onto her plate. "Say, this is a small town," she called over to Lily two tables away. "Surely you've heard something about last night? Was it an overdose? That girl?"

"Oh, gosh," said Lily as she stacked dirty plates. "I haven't heard anything. But I feel so awful for your friend Lester."

"Yes, his daughter," said Candace, glancing at her husband. "Can you believe it? Here, in town, in the witness protection program! What do you suppose she did? After all, I suppose Lester's blood, you know how he is, Giles…"

Candace went on, but Giles had closed his ears to his wife

long ago. He pretended he hadn't heard anything, and Candace turned back to Lily. The two women babbled on, their high female voices chattering like black-capped chickadees, their incessant calls becoming nothing but background noise to him.

Giles knew. Candace thought he was too stupid to know, too stupid to know anything, too stupid to know anything about her, but he knew.

He knew why she'd picked him—targeted him—and he knew she was too self-absorbed to realize he'd gone into the marriage fully aware. Aware of why she'd picked him, and aware of why he'd let her. He had been married before. He'd had a true love, the kind of love he suspected came along once in a lifetime. He'd already won his lottery, and didn't expect to win another. In Candace, he'd merely been looking for someone to warm the bed, occasionally cook some meals, someone to go to movies and dinner with so he didn't have to be entertained and eat alone. He knew she didn't care enough about him to get in the way of his plans, to have much to say at all, really, about how he lived his life. He knew she wanted his money, and he knew he didn't need that much himself. It was a tradeoff he went into willingly, no matter how much Candace may have thought she played him.

What he hadn't realized, though, was how much it would bother him to know he wasn't loved.

Or even liked.

And, to be honest, he was a little tired of it.

He also knew about Candace's affair with Lester.

He knew about it before they were married. Candace had been a fool to think the birders didn't talk. A reasonably attractive travel agent in Arizona, looking for a way out of her dismal life. She'd tested out a good number of the male birders, gone through them like a saltmarsh sparrow. Saltmarsh sparrows were considered among the most promiscuous of birds. Both male and female. Or a reed bunting, Giles thought. Rampant promiscuity. No, he thought, Candace was maybe more like the greater vasa parrot. Physically dominant—or so she thought—with often more than half a dozen partners.

She may have suspected that Giles knew about her affair with Lester before their marriage. But he also knew it had happened more than once since then. With Lester, and with others.

Lester was handsome in a way that transcended time. Lester was a god. Nothing like Giles. Lester had a burnished glow about him, like he was made of gold, lit from within. And he was smart. That's why they called him The Crow: his brain could work out any puzzle. Lester stood out physically and mentally. The women all swooned over him, even though he couldn't have cared less about them. He had to swat them away like flies sometimes. The fact that this girl who had died was Lester's daughter was a surprise, but not a shock. Lester probably had children all over the world. Women loved him. Men loved him. And yet somehow, Lester always stood alone.

Not like Giles. Giles was nothing special. Giles did not stand out. Giles fit in. He blended into the background. He could have put his patients to sleep just by talking to them. He was extraordinarily ordinary.

Lester had never settled down. Maybe because Lester couldn't settle, and never had to settle for someone he didn't love.

The woman they said was Branwen's mother, Giles didn't remember her. The birders were all talking about it, sharing notes, comparing timelines in their birding groups online, trying to figure it all out. The gossip was birdseed, scattered madly in the wind to a group of starving birds. The mother had been an addict, they said. Giles couldn't remember. It was possible. Even addicts loved Lester.

Did Giles envy Lester? Yes. People knew who he was. People talked about him. Giles had a face no one remembered. He had a life no one noticed. His first wife never had children, and he knew it was his fault. His sperm had undoubtedly been too unremarkable.

Lily and Candace continued to chirp on and it was all Giles could do not to get up and leave.

Maybe he would, soon.

Candace was an idiot. She'd picked him based on money, not realizing she had doomed herself to a life of invisibility, of nothingness. She was a narcissist, always wanting to be the center of attention, and she'd married the dullest man in the world, who gave her nothing but money.

If he had one regret, it was that he'd settled. He regretted not waiting for someone else to come alone. Or even no one else.

He looked out the window and saw only the vaguest reflection of himself in the pane. That's me, he thought. Only the vaguest reflection.

Giles had actually met Bridget on Thursday. He hadn't told anyone, and now that she was dead, no one else knew.

He'd been out on a walk, looking for the leucistic crow. Candace had been tired of pretending and had faked a headache just to get him to leave without her, so leave he did.

There was a trail along the river. That's where he'd met her.

She was standing near a park bench, holding binoculars, staring at the trees across the river.

"Are you looking for the crow?" he'd said, almost stunning himself with the sound of his own voice.

It made sense, now, knowing she was Lester's daughter. She, too, glowed.

What's more, she saw him. She didn't just look in his direction, like Candace did, like most people did. She saw him. His voice was soft, uncertain, unused, but still she turned toward it and smiled.

"Yes," she said. Her hair was dark, pulled back in a ponytail.

A short striped skirt and a blue or green shirt, though he knew someone else would have more technical names for what she wore. Candace would think it was too simple. Candace liked glitter, jewelry. Bling, the kids called it.

This girl shined without ornament. He couldn't look away.

"Found it?" he asked, his heart fluttering for the first time in years from something other than age. He was not used to talking. He was not used to being noticed.

"Not yet," she said. She pointed at the binoculars around his neck. "Are you looking, too?"

As his cheeks tightened, he thought, *this is what a smile feels like.* "Yes."

"You're a birder?" she asked. Encouraged. Waited for an answer. Listened.

"Yes," he said. "A birder. You?"

She paused. "I suppose I am," she said.

She didn't say anything more but Giles wanted her to keep talking. He scrambled for words, spelunking into the caverns of his mind for the long-forgotten art of conversation. "Are you from around here?" he asked. A weak effort, he knew, but he was rusty.

"Well, I'm here now," she said.

Giles smiled again. Again, the tightness in his cheeks. It felt good. "Me too," he said.

Later that afternoon, when he'd returned to the bed and breakfast, he hadn't been able to stop thinking about her. He wanted nothing more than to see her again.

THIRTEEN

After Max left, Megan sorted through her options. Next steps. The journals were sitting in the front hallway, calling to her, but something told her to hold off on that for now. There were so many questions, but first, she felt like she needed to know more about Bridget. Who she was. What she was like.

She could—and should—talk to Jace, of course, and Tatum, and the others in the theater. But something was telling her to start with Lester.

On a hunch, she decided to see if he might be at Emerson Falls, where they first met. Where he'd first been looking for the caramel crow.

Megan walked briskly to the falls, thinking as she did how much she loved this riverside trail. Maybe it was simply the whispering of the river as it whisked by, but she always felt she wasn't alone in this space. On this walk. Not just the squirrels scampering by or the eagles and hawks floating overhead, but the history of the place. How many other people had walked there. How many lovers had held hands as they gazed on the rushing river. How many people had sought solace at Addie's Park, staring out into the ripples of the water, looking up at the trees, as they sorted through their own inner turmoil. Walking through the veil of time, this place was never empty.

When she reached the main bridge at the falls, she saw Lester. Standing there, leaning on the railing of the bridge, staring at the waterfalls, but not seeing them. His gaze reached much deeper into his thoughts.

Megan approached him gently. Perhaps from decades spent watching for the tiniest movement in the trees, Lester sensed her presence immediately. He turned and gave her a sad smile.

"Found me," he said.

Another couple arrived and stood admiring the falls, taking selfies, laughing and talking loudly. While they were enjoying themselves, and rightly so, their presence was getting in the way of Megan having a private conversation with Bridget's father.

"There's a little nature trail," Megan said. "Do you want to walk with me?"

Lester pushed himself away from the bridge and waited for Megan to lead the way.

As they got farther from the falls, the roar of the water quickly diminished into a distant murmur. They stopped at a bench overlooking a turn in the river and sat.

"How are you doing?" Megan asked. She leaned sideways onto the back of the bench, turned toward this man who seemed caved in on himself, fallen.

A sound of pain escaped Lester's lips and he looked away, composing himself.

"I'm sorry. That's a ridiculous question," Megan said, trying to remember everything she knew about sitting with someone whose loved one had just died. The main thing was just to be present. At the same time, she had a job to do.

"I know it's a hard time … that's an understatement. I know

it's an unbearable time," Megan continued. "I want to help. We want to figure out what happened."

"She didn't do this," Lester said abruptly. "This wasn't her doing."

Megan nodded. Suicide was definitely something that would have to be ruled in or out. "The lab still has to come back with reports, but I know we want to look into every possibility." She paused. Where to begin? "Tell me about your daughter," she said.

Lester shook his head. Where to begin? "I wasn't around until a little later, when she was in grade school. Primary school. She was my best friend for those years. We were best buddies. Her mother was … her mother was busy a lot. So Bran and I would go on bike rides, we'd build forts in the woods out of branches, but there were never enough branches so the forts weren't that big. She'd sit inside the fort and I'd sit outside and she'd tell me to play the harmonica. But I didn't have a harmonica so I just pretended, humming and moving my hands in front of my mouth. She would laugh and laugh, so hard tears would be falling down her face." He took a deep breath and closed his eyes for a few minutes. Megan sat quietly, letting him take his time.

"She liked birds, too," Lester continued. "She knew she'd been named for my nickname. She loved crows and ravens. Some people hate them, you know. Think they're loud and pushy. But they're smart, so clever. She read books about crows and then would come tell me. 'Do you know, Daddy, that when people work with crows they wear masks because if they're mean to them the crows will remember them and will dive bomb them for the rest of their lives?' She was right. Crows have a very long memory. Crows are persistent. If crows had opposable thumbs, we'd all be in trouble. They'd take over the world." He chuckled lightly.

"Bran was an only child and had to amuse herself a lot. She

created whole worlds of invisible friends. That bothered me. I wanted her to have real friends. Then I finally remembered I never had many real friends, either, and I think I turned out okay." He tilted his head, like he was measuring this assessment and wasn't so sure it was accurate, but he wasn't going to correct it. "She used to put on plays, acting out every part herself. She'd charge a quarter, and make lemonade for the concessions stand, and then she'd use the money to buy groceries when her mother forgot." He dipped his head, looking down at his hands. "She took care of her mother more than her mother took care of her."

"Why didn't you stay?" The words slipped out of Megan's mouth even as she wanted to pull them back in. She hadn't meant it as judgment, just as curiosity. Still, there was no way for it not to sound unkind.

Lester felt it, too, the dagger to his heart that was present in the question. He flinched. "I couldn't, Megan," he said, shaking his head at himself. "Have you ever heard of restless leg syndrome?"

Megan nodded.

"That's me, but not my legs. My life. I tried to stay but I had to go. Should I have taken Bran with me? I don't know. Would she have been better off?" He shook his head again.

"Do you have other children?" Megan asked. "You're a good looking man. I'm sure you were popular with the ladies."

At this, Lester laughed loudly, a sudden unexpected sound. "Ha!" He said. "Looks mean nothing. Yes, you get chased. But do you know, it's a blessing and a curse. They saw me as a solution, not as a human with my own needs. They could never understand. But yes, a couple of other children."

"Do any of them have any … any bone to pick with Bridget? I mean Branwen? Anything at all?"

"No," Lester said quickly. "No."

A bird squawked overhead, and Lester's ears perked. "Red-tailed hawk, I believe," he said. He scanned the forest and the sky but the hawk was in hiding.

"Wingspan?" Megan asked.

"Ah, three or four feet," Lester said. "A good-sized bird." He looked at Megan, seeing her for the first time that day. "You might be a northern pygmy owl," he said, looking her up and down. "Fierce. Smart." He looked longer, then shook his head. "Or maybe a cockatoo."

Megan laughed. "Me? A cockatoo?"

"More playful than northern pygmy owls," he said. "Northern pygmy owls eat other birds."

"Oh," Megan said. "Yes, maybe more of a cockatoo." She laughed.

They heard voices, and soon the couple that had been taking selfies on the bridge earlier came into sight along the trail, talking animatedly. Megan and Lester waited for them to pass.

"So the witness protection program," Megan said finally.

"So the witness protection program," Lester repeated.

"Do you know much about it? Why your daughter was in it? Who would be looking for her?"

Lester shook his head. "Drugs," he said. "Big drug ring. She saw a man killed. She knew their secrets. She testified." He closed his eyes again, as if he could block out the reality of the present. Then he turned to Megan. "Do you think I made a mistake in coming here? Did I bring them with me?"

"Who?" Megan asked. "Did you bring who?"

"Whoever came and killed her."

A lump filled Megan's throat. The same thought had occurred to her. Had someone known of the relationship between Lester and Bridget, and followed him? But she couldn't bring herself to place blame. All he'd wanted was to see his daughter again. Who could blame him for that?

"She reached out," Lester said, trying to find words that would absolve himself, if he ever could. "She called out to me. 'Fair Raven.' She knew the rare bird was nearby. She knew I might be there. She was alone, Megan," he said, his words a plea. "She was alone. She wanted someone to talk to. I had to come. But in the end … I killed her."

"You killed her?" Megan said, her attention snapping to the man sitting beside her.

"I may as well have," Lester said. "I brought this on. This is all my fault."

"You don't know that," Megan said. "You don't."

Lester turned to Megan, his eyes swimming in water. "Please," he said, "please find out for sure."

Megan was overwhelmed with emotion, and she was relieved when her phone buzzed in her pocket. "It's Lily," she said, reading the text. "The caramel crow has been seen over near Addie's Park. That's back that way," she pointed, "by the river. On the river walk."

Lester nodded. "I saw it earlier today," he said. "The crow. I saw it on my way here. I sat and had a talk with it. I asked it who killed my Bran."

"Did it answer?" Megan asked.

Lester shook his head. "No."

FOURTEEN

When the U.S. Marshals come get you to sweep you away into the witness protection program, you don't get any warning. At least, I didn't. I guess that's because they want to save you from yourself. If you had any warning you might tell people, and that would defeat the whole purpose.

I had to pack, not much and very quickly, and they didn't let me bring any photos. No photos of people, anyway. Someone could recognize someone in a photo. Your cover would be blown. Next thing you'd be dead and it would be their fault for letting you bring a picture of someone you loved.

It doesn't much matter.

I'm here now.

Still alive.

They've brought me to a practically nonexistent town on a nice enough river. Emerson Falls, Washington. It seems okay. Out of the way. Not a place you'd find by accident. Not a place you'd go looking for someone. Hardly even a blip on the map.

There's a little park on the river. It has a little bench that faces out to the river, and I feel like it's mine. Like it was meant for me. My bench. My sanctuary.

According to a plaque on the bench, the park is named for the wife of the man who founded this town. Adeline Emerson. Addie. Adeline is kind of a nice name. Old fashioned, but sweet. She and I are both dead, in a way. I feel like she's welcomed me. Like Addie held out her hand and invited me to sit here, beside her. Told me she'd be here whenever I need her.

Why does it feel right now like all my friends are ghosts?

On the day they brought me to Emerson Falls, I went and sat at that bench for like two hours. A few runners and walkers went by on the trail in front of it. They waved and smiled but no one came over to say hello. That's okay. They were busy working out.

Maybe I'll take up running, too. Jogging, maybe. Or walking. I should do something. There's so much nature out here. I should get to know it. If I'm going to reinvent myself, I may as well have a healthy hobby.

They told me I had to pick a new name. They said if I use the same initials I have now—had—it might be easier for me to remember, not to slip up and reveal myself. I guess, like, if I go to sign my name and I start signing B for Branwen or something I still have a second to cover my mistake. So I went from Branwen Heybrook to Bridget Hill. I kind of like it. Bridget, like a bridge, between two lives. Gives me hope that maybe I can go back over the hill to the other side.

But. There's nothing on the other side anymore. There was just Joel. Maybe it's a one-way bridge. Anyway they've already changed my name so wherever that bridge goes, I'm Bridget now.

And Hill. I looked up last names starting with H, and Hill was near the top. Seems generic enough. Hard-to-find enough. Hunt is up near the top, too, but the last thing I wanted was to be hunted. Hill is nice. Rolling hills, green hills, hills that when you climb them let you see farther than you could see from down below.

It's a strange feeling. Branwen Heybrook was unique. On Facebook, I was the only one.

I guess that's why they won't let me keep that name.

But I wonder. I keep wondering.

If I'm not Branwen Heybrook, then who am I?

What is it that makes me, me?

To change my identity, how much of that do I have to give up? Is giving up my name enough? Or do I have to give up more? Do I have to give up my essence? My soul?

There are a million Bridget Hills on Facebook. You just keep scrolling and scrolling and scrolling, more results pop up and then more and then more. There's no one definition of what it means to be Bridget Hill. Young and old, every race, Bridget Hill can be anyone. Now I'm one of the masses.

I know a person isn't their name. But it's unsettling to give it up. I'm no longer Branwen Heybrook. Now I'm a bridge and a hill. I'm part of the landscape. I'm invisible, which is what we all want. Which is what the marshals want, really. Is that my identity now? My destiny? To see but not be seen?

Maybe it's a good thing. A blessing, an opportunity most people don't get. A chance to let go of anything that was clinging to Branwen that I no longer wanted. Traits, habits, assumptions, expectations. It's all gone. Now I get to transform. Now I get to choose. Now I can be anyone. Maybe now I can be who I'm really meant to be, without all that baggage. Without the past. Maybe it'll be fun to become someone new.

A rose by any other name would smell as sweet. Shakespeare. Am I still Branwen inside? My father's fair raven?

The fair raven is gone.

He was a great dad, until he checked out. I guess I'm older now and I know he loved me, still loves me. The older I get the more I realize that adults don't know everything. When I was a kid I assumed that when I got to a certain age, that'd be it, I'd know everything, I'd have it all figured out. But maybe no one ever figures it out. Maybe they just sort of settle into a comfort with not knowing. Or maybe they give up.

I guess that's where forgiveness comes in.

I sent my dad a letter, through the marshals. Told him what I could. They said they'd mail it on. I know they opened it. I don't know if he got it.

Maybe if I'd been Bridget all along, I would have fit in better. Been more popular. Known the right things to say. Would have known how to navigate the world, how not to get myself into a mess trying to save everyone but myself.

Maybe I would have belonged.

I've always been on the outside. Have I found the key to the inner circle? Is it just a name, is that enough? Will they let me in? Or will they somehow know I'm an intruder?

My job now is to figure out how to blend in without losing myself.

I don't know where to begin.

At some point, they'll take me back to testify about everything I know about Joel, the drugs, the ring, the people. They'll want me to talk about everything that happened on the day Joel died. I can still see it all, clear as day.

I see it even more clearly at night. In my nightmares.

I'll put on my Branwen suit again for a few days and bring up her memories and pour out her heart, and then I'll take Branwen off again and be Bridget. If we do it right, everything I've ever lived, every bit of who I've been, is gone and buried now. My past doesn't exist.

Blessing and curse.

Either way, it's my truth.

I feel like I've fallen into a black hole and there's no way out.

FIFTEEN

Up on Megan's balcony, a soft, sporadic autumn wind lifted the pages of Bridget's journal on Megan's lap. She'd been reading since she'd returned from the waterfalls. Interspersed with more traditional journal entries were random writings, poems, some attempts at a scratchy sort of art here and there. Doodles laced the edges of the pages. More than once, Bridget had written character sketches of women in their early twenties. Megan imagined Bridget trying on these personalities like clothes. Will this person fit me? Could this be who I am?

But in the first few months of her time in Emerson Falls, at least, Bridget had revealed nothing that seemed in any way helpful to uncovering who might have wanted to hurt her. Megan sensed a hesitance. A holding back. As though even as she wrote, in the privacy of her new home in a tiny town in Washington, barely a blip on the map, she was always looking over her shoulder. Waiting for the moment when someone would find her out.

Who had found her out?

Had Lester led someone to Emerson Falls, or had someone else found Bridget on their own?

Megan closed Bridget's journal and ran her hand over the cover. Most of the journals Max had left behind for her to read were just college-ruled spiral-bound notebooks in a myriad of colors. But this first one had been selected with more care. The cover was almost soft, moleskine maybe, a color somewhere between summer sky and glacial river, with a sort of scrollwork design in a darker shade. The artwork, while ambiguous, made Megan think of a river. Had Bridget seen it, too? Having spent more than an hour reading Bridget's thoughts and musings, Megan felt intimately close with her and wanted to ask her questions. She wanted, most of all, to ask forgiveness for her transgressions, and permission to continue. It felt both sinful and exhilarating to read someone else's diaries. Like she'd been given entrance to a forbidden room.

And what, exactly, was the lure? Megan couldn't help but wonder. Deep within the lines, hidden in the pages, what answers might she find? Not just the evidence and the clues, but answers about humanity. About herself. In words written for no other reason than to get them out of her head, what had Bridget revealed?

The truth, Megan thought. What goes on in our minds can't be known by anyone else. Everything inside our heads remains an eternal secret.

"Until we write it down," Megan said to the river. Are we the person we reveal to others, or are we the person we never show to the world? Which side of us is real? Megan drank the last bit of coffee in her cup. It had gone cold. Megan put the green-blue notebook on top of the others and stared out at the river. "We all just want to know that we're normal," she said. "That we're not alone in our strangest thoughts."

She sighed.

"What I need," she said, standing abruptly and picking up her empty cup, "is to find out more about Bridget." Who was she? That is, who was she in Emerson Falls? While the drug conspiracy connection seemed to be the most obvious motive, they couldn't focus only on Branwen as a witness protection client. They also had to focus on Bridget. The person who had shown up in Emerson Falls. Whatever person Branwen had chosen to transform into.

The theater, then, Megan thought. She'd start there.

Much to Megan's surprise, the theater was buzzing, and not with police. The first person Megan spotted that she knew was Tatum, on stage, touching up a wall with some paint. Tatum stood and looked over her work while Megan took in the scene. When Megan had first seen Tatum, what had come to mind was the description of Nancy Drew's friend Bess: "pleasingly plump." Tatum was soft, curvy, small and compact. Maybe five feet tall, maybe not quite. Her blue hair looked like it hadn't been combed before she'd put it into short, messy pigtails. Tatum wore a tight black t-shirt with two bright yellow cat's eyes on the front, and her black jeans were strewn with holes. Whether the jeans came pre-made with the tears or Tatum had worn them through with time, Megan didn't know.

"Tatum," Megan called out as she climbed the stairs to the stage.

Tatum turned and stared at Megan, her expression not changing.

"Hey," Megan said. She looked around the room. The actors were there, many seated in the third and fourth rows, talking intensely, some with faces haggard from lack of sleep. Other cast and crew milled about alone or in smaller groups. A few were laughing lightly at their conversations, but for the most part their looks were somber. "I guess I thought you guys would cancel for tonight?"

Tatum pursed her lips. "Jace said no. 'The show must go on.' He literally said that." She wiped the tip of the paintbrush she was holding on a rag. When she scratched her nose, a tiny bit of paint transferred from her finger. She looked at Megan and tilted her head, waiting for a reaction.

"Oh," said Megan, taking this in. "I suppose there were lots of tickets sold. Reimbursing would be a nightmare."

"It's not like she was an actor. The show can go on without her," Tatum said. Something in the way she said it made Megan think she was repeating words rather than stating her own mind.

"How's everyone doing?" Megan asked. "Has there been any news?" She assumed if there had been word from the lab, Max would have told her, but sometimes news spread faster in back channels.

"I'd say everyone's doing how you'd expect?" Tatum said, turning the statement into a question. She put a hand on her hip, now transferring paint to her black jeans.

"Yeah, bad question, sorry." Megan looked around the set. She saw the bench, the one where Liesl and Rolf would declare that their sixteen- and seventeen-year-old love would go on forever, and where later Maria would declare her baffled disbelief to the Captain that somewhere in her youth or childhood, she must have done something good. "Can we sit?" Megan said. "Do you have time?"

"I'm doing Bridget's job too, now," Tatum said.

Megan wondered if Tatum knew Bridget hadn't been the stage manager's real name, but she decided it wasn't important at the moment. Hoping Tatum would follow her, she walked to the bench.

Tatum looked around and shrugged, then sat next to Megan.

"Tell me about Bridget," Megan said. "What, exactly, happened last night?" The scene had been cleared away and all was cleaned up, so Megan knew the forensics team was done. The show must go on indeed.

Tatum rolled her eyes. "I went over this with the police," she said.

"I know," Megan said. "Can you tell me, too? I'm helping them."

Tatum looked around the room to see who was there. Who was listening.

"It was after the show," Tatum started.

Megan tried to quell her impatience. Obviously it was after the show, she thought. But then again, was it obvious? Max would remind her to assume nothing.

"Are you sure it was after the show?" Megan said. "Had you seen Bridget alive during the show?"

Tatum's eyebrows twitched. "Well, no. But I saw her alive before the show," she said defensively.

"Where were you during the show?" Megan asked.

"Backstage," Tatum said. "Wardrobe. With the actors as they changed."

"And during intermission?" Megan said. "Did you see Bridget then?"

Tatum brightened. "Yes. She was talking ... I saw her talking to the security guy. I don't know his name. He's just here for the performance nights."

"Is he here right now?" Megan asked.

Tatum scanned the room, holding her hand against her forehead to shield her eyes from the stage lights. "I don't see him," she said, "but it's hard to see."

Megan wrote a note in her small notebook, reminding herself to find and talk to the security guy.

"And after that? After intermission, did you see her again during the show?" Megan asked.

"During the show I'm a little busy," Tatum said.

Megan nodded. "So that's a no?"

"That's a no," Tatum said, rolling her eyes. She tugged on one of her pigtails absentmindedly.

"Okay. So you didn't see Bridget alive after intermission?"

"I guess not."

"When did you see her next?" Megan asked, as gently as she could. There was simply no delicate way to talk about death and murder.

Tatum pointed to the wings, offstage, where Bridget had been found, in a small space tucked behind a curtain. "A while after the show was over. She was over there," she said. A cloud of memory covered her eyes and she blinked.

"And ... she'd ... she was lying down?"

"We were cleaning up after the performance. The party was going on downstairs, and most people had been gone for a while already, but ... I was still up here. Getting the set and costumes ready for today so I wouldn't have to come in early. I'm not the one who found her. It was Jace. She was behind a prop, but he saw her foot sticking out. She'd thrown up. She was lying in it ... next to it. Jace was with her, trying to get her to wake up. He turned to me and said she was cold and told me to get a blanket. Then he pulled out his phone and called 911."

"Did he try CPR on her or anything?" Megan said.

"No ... I think she was still breathing. She wasn't ... she wasn't dead yet."

Megan took this in. "Okay. Tell me about the other people in the theater that night. I know you were busy. But did you notice anyone unusual? Anyone who wasn't supposed to be there, any audience members acting suspiciously, anything out of the ordinary?"

Tatum rolled her eyes again. "It's a theater. There are weird people all over."

"Did you see anyone backstage who wasn't supposed to be there?"

Tatum shook her head.

"Anyone odd in the audience?"

"I didn't bother looking, really."

Megan pursed her lips and thought. "Okay, the security guy. You didn't know him. Who hired him, do you know?"

Tatum shrugged. "Probably Jace," she said. "I don't know, though."

Megan squinted, trying to think of what else she should ask. "Did Bridget have a boyfriend? Or girlfriend? Or any jealous exes? Was there anyone who didn't like her?"

An exasperated smirk scrunched half of Tatum's face. "She and Jace seemed to spend a lot of time together," she said. "You should ask him."

"I will," Megan said. "Do you know where he is?"

"No idea," Tatum said, standing. The interrogation was over.

Megan followed Tatum's lead and stood as well. "Thank you, Tatum. If you think of anything else," she pointed to the library, "you know where to find me."

Tatum nodded, unimpressed, and returned to work.

"That was a real help," Megan said quietly to the now-empty stage. Had she really learned anything useful? Maybe that she needed to talk to the security guy, and Jace. But beyond that …

"What we need," she said, "is a meeting of the minds. Time to call in the troops."

SIXTEEN

Luckily for Megan, her designated troops were all available and eager to join her. "And not just because you suggested wine with lunch," Lily said when she RSVP'd to Megan's group text. "Be there in a minute!"

By the time Megan got to Rae's, Lily and Max were already at their favorite large corner booth, where they could generally talk without being overheard.

Rae nodded at Megan as she walked in the door. "Busy, but I'll come by," Rae said, carrying a tray of burgers to another table. "You want lunch?"

"Lunch and a glass of white, please!" Megan called out.

"I'll bring a bottle," Rae said, winking.

Megan shrugged off her light jacket and slid into the seat next to Max. "Hey, Chief," she said. "Any news yet from the labs?"

"Nothing yet. It's not like the movies. It can take some time. But the FBI agent should be coming in later this afternoon," he said, checking his watch. "Landing at SeaTac right about now, so a few more hours."

"Do you know anything about him or her?" Megan asked.

"Are we getting a him or a her?" Lily asked. "A Scully or a Mulder?"

Owen arrived just as Lily asked, and he slipped into the seat next to her. "Hopefully a Scully," he said. "Much more efficient."

"What!" Lily said, scowling at Owen. "Scully was the worst. Not a scientist at all. If she'd been a real scientist she wouldn't have kept denying evidence—*including her own alien baby.*"

Rae set a bottle of wine and four glasses on the table, raising her eyebrows at the part of the conversation she'd overheard. "Who had an alien baby?" she said. "I thought I was on top of everything in this town?"

"They're *X-Files* fans," Megan whispered to Rae. "They will never agree on this." She smiled at Owen and Lily, who were now scowling at Megan in response to her mocking their favorite show.

Lily reached for the bottle of wine and started pouring. "Max, are you on or off duty right now?"

"On," Max said. "None for me right now."

"That has to be the worst part of on-call jobs," Megan said. "No wine or beer or cocktails while you're on call." She held out a glass, which Lily filled.

"We'll go out some other time and make up for it," Lily said with a reassuring look at Max, who did not seem terribly worried. Lily poured wine for the rest of them, then poured a glass of water for Max. "So, what's up, Megan?"

Megan took a sip of the wine. "Wasn't it Hemingway who said 'write drunk, edit sober'? I wouldn't be surprised if that suggestion would hold for coming up with murder theories, right? I mean, a loose mind must brainstorm better?"

"Not exactly what they teach at the academy," Max laughed. "But the idea isn't without merit."

"Well, we won't get carried away," Megan said. "I just wanted to gather our hive mind together to see what anyone has seen or heard. See if there are any dots we've already found, that are just waiting to be connected. I talked with Tatum at the theater today; didn't get much from her. But I do need to talk with the security guy, and Jace."

"I talked with the security guy this morning," Max said. "He didn't have much insight. He did mention that there were several people at the dress rehearsal, though, people he didn't recognize. When I asked him if he thought he'd recognize most locals, though, he said no."

"Hmm," said Megan. "I should have asked Tatum about that. I'll see if I can get a list from Jace or someone of anyone who was at the dress rehearsal. You never know, could have been a stalker."

"I think a few of my guests were there, actually," said Lily. "That Giles went, I think, though his wife didn't. She was annoyed with him the next morning for going without her. And a couple of others. I'll see if I can find out."

Max nodded.

Rae brought over a platter and set it on the edge of the table, then distributed plates full of luscious-looking salads to each of the foursome.

"What have we here?" Megan said, ogling the food.

"Spinach, pear, and Gorgonzola salad with candied pecans," Rae said, pleased with herself. "Tried it the other night and it was a hit."

"It looks delicious," Lily said, digging in with her fork.

"It is delicious," Max said through his stuffed mouth. "Thank you, Rae."

"For you, anything," Rae said, mocking a swoon in Max's direction. In Rae's eyes, Max could do no wrong. "So what are we discussing today?" she said, flipping a towel over her shoulder and slipping the empty platter under her arm.

"Clues," Megan said. "Dots. Seeing what we have. So. Anyone?"

Owen opened his mouth to speak, but then hesitated. Finally, he started. "So, I don't know if this is relevant …"

"Give it to us anyway," Megan said, chasing a pecan around her plate with her fork. "Better more information than not enough."

"It wasn't the night of the murder," Owen said, still seeming to debate whether what he had to say was important. "But it was unusual."

Max nodded encouragingly. "Let us decide."

"Well, I was headed home a little after one in the morning. I was up on the highway. Just west of that new restaurant, Bezauberung," Owen said.

"Traitor," said Rae, with a wink to Owen.

"What were you doing out at Bezauberung at one in the morning?" Lily asked with an innocent smile.

"It's not important," Owen said.

"Let us decide," Megan said, nodding encouragingly.

Owen blushed. "I was on a date. Anyway, I was on the highway—"

"A *date*," Megan said, sharing a delighted glance with Lily. "Anyone we know?"

"No," said Owen. "Anyway, I was driving—"

"What's his name?" Lily said, wiggling her eyebrows at Owen. "First date? Second date?"

Owen leveled a glare at Lily. "No."

Megan turned to Lily. "What an odd name. 'No.'" She looked at Owen. "Is that a family name? Like, he's named after Uncle No, the old curmudgeon that everyone couldn't help but love?"

Owen raised his eyebrows and looked to Max for help.

"It does seem like an odd name," Max said. "Is he cute?"

"You are not helping," Owen said, shaking his head.

"The more information we have, the better," Max said, his dimples deepening in his cheeks.

"*Anyway*," Owen said, his face beet red. "As I was saying, I was driving up on the highway, headed home. And I saw a car broken down on the side of the road. Well, it was on the side of the road, anyway. I assumed it was broken down."

"Oh," said Lily. "That must have been Simon. Wednesday night?"

Owen nodded. "Wednesday night, yes."

"You were out on a date on a Wednesday night?" Megan said. She turned to Max. "This must be serious."

"I swear, you people …" Owen said.

"We're sorry," Lily said. "Go on."

"I'm not actually sorry," Megan whispered with a giggle.

Owen rolled his eyes. "The odd thing was not the car broken down. What seemed unusual was there was a guy walking down the road away from the car, toward Emerald Falls, carrying a big backpack. I mean, it wasn't illegal or anything. But it was late, so I noticed."

"Did you get a look at the guy?" Max said. "Or did you talk to him?"

Owen shrugged his shoulders. "I suppose I should have stopped to help, but it was late, and …"

"And you were daydreaming about your extraordinary date with No," Megan said knowingly.

Lily laughed. "This is probably why Owen doesn't tell us about his dates," she said.

"You think?" Owen said, but the slightest hint of a smile reassured the others that he wasn't overly offended. "Yeah, I couldn't see much. It was dark, obviously. I'd say dark hair, a leather jacket maybe, average size guy, a little toward the short and slim side. That's about all I saw. I was, after all," the side of his lip tilted up, "mooning a bit about No."

"Ahhhhh!" said Megan. "Oh my goodness, after we get this mystery solved I am digging in to find out everything I can about No. But that does sound like Simon. Lily, do you remember him going out in the middle of the night?"

Lily shook her head. "I would have been sound asleep by then, and guests all have their own keys. I didn't notice a thing."

"I suppose he probably just needed his clothes and stuff," Megan said. "But why go in the middle of the night?"

"Bad sleeper?" said Max. "Insomnia? Needed some fresh air?"

"Are they still fixing his car, Lily? Do you know?" Megan asked.

Lily shook her head. "I haven't asked. I should have! Such a bad hostess. It's the weekend now, though. Maybe he has to wait until Monday."

"Hmmm," said Megan. "Hmmmm."

"Hmmm, you have an idea?" said Max.

"No," said Megan. "Hmmm, I have no idea on that one. I'll see if I can figure out a way to casually run into him and interrogate him. There's also another couple, Lily, they know Lester, right?"

"Yes," said Lily. "Candace and Giles Levine. Fellow birders. They don't seem terribly keen on each other, though, I'll tell you that much. He's just recently retired, and I get the sense they were trying to save the marriage, but maybe aren't having a lot of luck."

"Is she retired, too?" Megan said. "What kind of work do they do? Where are they from?"

"I don't think she's worked for a while. He just retired from a career in anesthesiology. I think they're from Arizona, but I'll have to double check. They're staying through Monday, if I remember right. Simon is just here until the car's fixed."

"Hmmm," said Megan.

"Hmmmmm," said Lily.

"Don't forget, Megan," Max said. "Lester. Just because you like him doesn't mean he's not a suspect." He looked her square in the eye.

"I know, I know," Megan said. "But I really think he's one of the least likely. Don't you?"

"He came here just to see her," Max said. "He's the only one who we know for sure was here specifically to see Bridget. My gut says you're probably right. But we can't rule him out."

"Yes, I know," Megan said. She recalled again how she interrupted Bridget and Lester's conversation in the hallway. She'd been thinking she had broken apart some father-daughter time, but had she, in fact, halted an early attempt at a crime? No, she couldn't believe Lester had meant his daughter any harm. She would keep him in mind, but as far as his being her first suspect, she just didn't believe it. "The show tonight hasn't been canceled, by the way," Megan continued. "I thought it would be, but Tatum said Jace didn't want to. What do we know about Jace?" She looked around the table.

"He's pretty new to town, is all I know," said Lily.

Rae had been so quiet that Megan had almost forgotten the restaurant owner had been standing behind her. She spoke up now. "Jace and Bridget came into the pub a few times together," she said. "Always seemed pretty close."

"Like dating close? Were they holding hands or making out or anything?" Megan asked.

"None of that," Rae said. "But the way they leaned in toward each other. You can just tell, right?"

"They worked together," Max said. "Could have been discussing work things, away from the theater."

"Could have," Rae said. "But that's not the vibe I got."

"Did he ever pay for both of them?" Lily asked. "That might indicate a date."

"Or a work lunch," Owen said. He looked at Megan. "No one gets angry if their boss pays for their meal, I'm just saying."

Megan laughed. "Do we know any more about him? He was the one who found Bridget. Or at least, he's the one Tatum saw with her first. I suppose it's possible someone else was with her and left, or that she was alone when she fainted."

Max chimed in. "I've talked with Jace, but by all means, you should talk with him too, see what he tells you. He told me that he had been downstairs to check on the party, then came up-stairs to finish shutting down the theater for the night, when he saw a leg behind a prop. He looked, and it was Bridget. Very soon after that, he said, Tatum found the both of them."

"Do you get the feeling … I guess this is just speculation. I feel like Tatum either doesn't like Jace, or really likes Jace," Megan said.

"Jealous, you mean? Jealous, maybe, of Bridget and Jace? If they were a thing?" asked Lily.

"That's exactly what I'm wondering," Megan said.

"Worth asking around about," Max said. He looked at his watch again. "I had better go. With the FBI agent coming in, I want to get some things ready first."

"And I want to read more in Bridget's journals," Megan said. "In case the agent tries to take them from me. Okay, I'm going to try to find that couple, Candace and Giles, and also Simon. If any of you see one of them, text me! And talk to them! See if they let slip that they murdered anyone recently or anything."

"Got it," said Owen. "Beat confession out of random tourists. Noted."

"Good job," said Megan. "That's the spirit!" She turned to Max. "Let us know what the agent says, if you can?"

"If I can," Max said.

"All right, then. I'm off to try to track down Simon. Or the Levines. Or someone." Megan called out to Rae, who had gone to help another customer. "Rae! Put all this on my tab!" she said, indicating all the food and drink on the table. Megan winked at Owen. "You can pay me back in gossip. I want details." She waved at her troops and set off to find whoever she could find.

SEVENTEEN

Megan stepped outside the pub and took a deep breath of the crisp fall air. The few deciduous trees had started to turn; the nights were starting to get cooler even as the days were still warm. The sun sparkled on the town. Down at the river, she knew the sunlight would be dancing on the water, almost blinding at times.

"That's where I'd be," Megan said to the street. If she weren't a resident, and if she didn't have a car, she'd be somewhere down by the river or at the falls. Mostly because the library was closed today and there wasn't much else to do without a car to get you out of town. Emerson Falls, she thought, was a great place to live, but maybe less exciting to visit. But she wouldn't want to live anywhere else.

The brightness of the day buoyed her step as she rushed down the road toward the library. Her plan, as she created it on the fly, was to walk the riverfront trail from its start at the library, up to the falls, trace the nature trail route at the falls, and then return to the library, crossing her fingers the whole time that she might meet one of her suspects along the way.

She passed Lily's B&B on her route and slowed to a crawl as she went by, peering into windows as best she could without being conspicuous. She knew the accommodations were full, but several cars were gone for the day, probably out sightseeing. Looking over her shoulder, she traipsed through the grounds of the B&B, just in case Simon or the Levines might be outside soaking in the sunshine. But the yard was quiet, its chairs and tables empty. The only sounds were the birds, chirping and calling out to her.

"Do you know where anyone went?" Megan asked softly, looking up to the sky.

The birds did not reply.

"Really not helpful, birds," she whispered. These birds were not Cinderella's birds, apparently, and she was not Cinderella.

Megan continued down the road, gravel crunching under her feet. She ran upstairs at the library to grab a day bag and a bottle of water, and then headed outside again along the riverside trail.

The trail was quiet, peaceful, and Megan ambled slowly, enjoying the day. The river was running end-of-summer low; mid-stream boulders that were underwater in the height of the river flow were now peeking above the surface. Megan loved to watch the way the river changed through the seasons. Always different, even while always the same.

The calm of the day lulled Megan into an almost meditative state. But just before she reached Addie's Park, Megan stopped abruptly and gasped. There, on the trail, strolling along with its black tufted ears and distinctive stubby tail, was a lynx. Megan stood as still as possible, watching in awe. She knew there were Canada lynx in the area, but she'd never actually seen one. What had brought this one out into the open? It didn't look like it was hungry; in fact, it seemed quite fluffy and healthy. It was about twice the size of a domestic cat; its paws were enormous. More than anything Megan wanted to cuddle with it, but she knew better. Megan knew the lynx was unlikely to hurt her unless it felt threatened, so she simply waited, breathing slowly, hoping it wouldn't run away.

Sensing Megan's presence, the lynx stopped and turned to look. It met Megan's eyes, and Megan almost couldn't breathe. She knew it was ridiculous to put human emotions into animals—or was it? Were animals so different from humans? Surely some animals felt some emotions. Did this one see her? Would it recognize her if she saw it again? More likely it would recognize her than the other way around, Megan thought. Animal instincts. Humans liked to believe humans were so much more advanced, but it was dogs, not humans, who could smell cancer. Elephants, not humans, that would flee to higher ground before humans and all their science could detect any hint of a tsunami. Was it so far-fetched, then, to believe this lynx could see into Megan's heart?

The lynx was looking straight at her and yet through her, like it was completely unconcerned with her presence. Megan felt a flutter of pleasure, wanting to believe the lynx could tell she wished it no harm. The lynx's ears twitched and its head turned away from Megan. Something more interesting had caught its attention.

"Be safe," Megan whispered as the lynx turned and padded away, softly, slowly, headed toward Emerson Falls.

After it was well out of sight, Megan walked to the bench at Addie's Park and sat. She pulled out her bottle of water and took a sip, then turned on her phone and opened the browser app.

What does a lynx symbolize? she typed in the search bar. She read through the various answers. Awareness, confidence, intuition, trust, playfulness, patience, and on and on.

When Megan got to the last sentence, the hair went up on the back of her neck:

The ability to see what others cannot see; to uncover secrets. No secrets will remain unknown.

Megan didn't find anyone at Emerson Falls, even though she walked the full trail system twice. Eventually, she admitted defeat and headed back toward the library.

And, finally, she was rewarded. There, sitting at Addie's bench, not so far from where the lynx had made its rare and spectacular appearance, was Simon.

"Hello!" Megan called out, putting on her Ambassador to Emerald Falls hat. "Simon, am I remembering right?" *As if we weren't just talking about you*, she thought. *See me being all sleuthy and sly?*

"Yes," said Simon, squinting at Megan, trying to remember her. "We met … at that bar?"

"The pub," Megan said. "Rae's pub. The night your car broke down. Have they fixed it yet?"

Simon spread his arms out, as if to say *I'm still here, can't you see?* "Not yet. Great timing on my part, breaking down in the middle of nowhere on a weekend."

Simon was taking up the middle of the bench, arms now fully laid out over the top of the backrest, so Megan leaned against a fence post. She nodded out toward the river. "I mean, I'm biased, but I'd say there are worse places to get stuck. Have you had a chance to look around?"

"Yeah," Simon said. "People have been nice."

"There's a show at the theater," Megan said, testing the waters, dipping her toes in. "*The Sound of Music*. The theater is brand new and this is the first production. We're all pretty excited." As she spoke she carefully watched his face for any change in expression. She thought he'd blinked more than a person would normally blink when hearing about a random new theater. Or was the sun in his eyes?

"Yeah," he said. He looked away from Megan. "I saw it last night." He then looked at Megan, and he seemed to be studying her as much as she'd studied him. "A girl died?" he said.

"Yes," Megan said. "A young woman named Bridget." Would her killer have known her as Branwen? Megan wasn't sure which name she should have used.

"Sad," he said, still watching Megan.

His unwavering gaze felt like an invasion. Megan's skin started to crawl and she shifted her weight from one leg to the other. "Yes," she said. "Horrible."

"Do they know the cause?" Simon asked. "I heard there were questions?"

"They don't know yet," Megan said. "The labs can be so slow, I guess." She suddenly wondered, if Simon tried to attack her, would the lynx somehow know and come to her rescue?

Simon shook his head. "I suppose in a place like this, it's so much harder. Small town, everyone's close, I imagine. Everyone knows everyone."

Megan nodded, a wave of guilt washing over her as she remembered how she'd been thinking—after how many years?—that she should have had Bridget up for coffee. Why had she never done that? Was life in Emerson Falls so busy she couldn't afford half an hour with a neighbor?

"Yeah," Megan said softly. "She was sweet." Megan chided herself in her mind for her dishonesty. She hardly knew anything about Bridget. Had she felt safe in Emerson Falls? Did she have friends? Who did she ask when she needed someone to water her plants and get her mail? Megan suddenly had a craving to get back to those journals.

"How long are you here for?" Megan asked. "Will they have your car fixed soon?"

Simon shrugged. "They say Monday, but that mechanic didn't seem too concerned about time."

"Where did you take your car?" Megan said.

"A-A-Art's Collision Repair," Simon laughed. "I guess they wanted to be at the beginning of the phone book."

Megan smiled. "Phone books," she said. "There's a relic for you. Yeah, you're right, A-A-Art isn't the fastest guy in town, but he's the only guy in town."

At this, Simon gave a hearty chortle. "Good one," he said. "Not the fastest, but the only one." He shook his head, smiling.

"What exactly happened to your car?" Megan said. "Talk about bad timing. And you had to walk so far." She wanted to know why he'd walked back out there in the middle of the night, but other than just accusing him of it, she wasn't sure how to bring the subject up.

He lifted his shoulders and let them fall. "I've walked farther," he said. "It wasn't too bad."

"If there's anything in your car that you need," Megan said, her heart racing a bit, "I'm happy to take you over to A-A-Art's to get it." She tried to keep her gaze level and casual.

Simon paused for a second, and raised his eyes. "Nope," he said. "Got everything I need."

"Of course," said Megan, her skin crawling again. *Drat*, she thought. *Fail.*

A noise on the trail behind Megan caught Simon's attention, and his eyes widened. Megan stiffened. Was the lynx back? Was it about to pounce on her? Or on Simon? If it was aiming to pounce on her, would Simon just let it?

"Hey," said Simon.

Megan's fear morphed into confusion. Was Simon talking to the lynx? She turned, slowly, so as not to alarm the lynx. Instead, she saw Tatum.

"Tatum!" Megan said, almost laughing as a surge of unneeded adrenaline dissipated throughout her body. "Hey!"

Tatum looked from Megan to Simon and back, and then

raised an eyebrow at Simon.

"Hey," Tatum said. To Simon, she said, "Sorry I'm late."

Late? Megan thought. So this was an arranged meeting? "Oh, you two know each other?" Megan said.

Simon nodded slowly, his lips lifting at the side. "We met the other night."

Tatum smiled a tiny smirk, and Megan thought she knew what Simon meant by *met*. "The other night? Last night at the show?"

"No, Thursday night at dress rehearsal," Tatum said. "Simon came by."

"Oh," Megan said, her brain taking in this news. Simon had been at dress rehearsal. Simon had met Tatum. "That reminds me, Tatum. I wanted to ask you if you had any list or anything of who all was at the dress rehearsal? It was open to the public, wasn't it?"

"It was," Tatum said, "but mostly it was just the kids' families. The kid actors."

"And Simon," Megan said, trying to press Tatum to remember anyone else.

"Yeah, well, and Simon. And a couple other guys I didn't know. The one, Lester, who says he's her dad, and another old guy."

Megan looked at Simon. He was staying at the same B&B as the Levines. He would know them. "Simon, was that Giles Levine? Did you notice him there?"

Simon's lip curled and Megan again got the feeling that a lynx was about to pounce on her. "Yeah, it was that Giles guy, the anesthesiologist." He sounded out each syllable of *anesthesiologist* slowly, like he was either trying to get the word right, or mocking it somehow.

"Was his wife there?" Megan said.

"Nah," Simon said. "She doesn't like him." He laughed. "It's mutual."

Megan tucked this information away to decipher later. "Do you know if Giles saw Bridget, or talked with her?" she asked.

"Yeah," Simon said. "He was there early. Saw him talking with her for a while."

"Did it seem friendly?" Megan asked.

"Did it seem friendly or did it seem like he was about to murder her?" Simon grinned maliciously. "It seemed like he was more friendly than she was, that's what I'll say." He looked at Tatum and patted the seat on the bench beside him. "Come sit, darlin'," he said.

Megan took that as her cue to leave. She noted that if Simon had seen Giles at the theater early, that meant that Simon was at the theater early, too. Why had both of them been there so early? Did Giles know Bridget? Megan was starting to feel like she needed to create a chart of who knew whom. It was all getting quite convoluted.

On her way back to the library, Megan texted Lily.

Simon is at Addie's Park with Tatum, she wrote. *Have you cleaned his room?*

Lily wrote back in her signature series of quick texts.

Yes...

Or have I?

Is there something in there I need to re-clean?

Megan texted back.

I'm not suggesting you should look in his room for that bag Owen saw him carrying, and I'm certainly not suggesting you should look inside the bag to see what's in it.

Of course not, Lily wrote.

I would never.

Be right back.

Megan walked briskly back to the library grounds, stopping at the collection of benches by the river to sit and think, and to wait for the message she knew Lily would send as soon as possible.

She was not disappointed. Within a few minutes Lily's texts were flying in.

Megan!

I'm not saying I looked

but there's a bag in Simon's room

that he didn't have with him when we saw him at Rae's

and by some bizarre chance it spilled open when I went to vacuum

there were some gym clothes and shoes

and a box

that also just happened to fall open

and Megan I am no expert

but I think what was inside

was DRUGS!!!

EIGHTEEN

Megan felt a chill spread over her. Drugs? She remembered the way she'd felt around Simon back at Addie's Park. Was Simon dangerous? Did Tatum know? Was Lily at risk, harboring a criminal in her bed and breakfast?

She texted back to Lily:

Wait, tell me what you saw.

After a few moments, Lily replied:

Plastic baggies

Some with white powder

some with gel caps with white powder inside

Also some bags with what looked like weed

Pot

Grass

Whatever the kids are calling it these days

Fear was spreading through Megan.

Don't joke, she wrote. *I'm worried. We have to tell Max.*

Lily replied quickly:

I'm joking because it's strange

Megan answered:

Did you put everything back?

Yes, Lily wrote. *Just as I found it.*

Okay, Megan replied. *When he comes back, pretend everything is normal. I'll text Max.*

Lily wrote back cheerfully:

I run a B&B

I'm used to treating people like they're normal

Even when they're bonkers!

No problem!

Gotta go

Phone call incoming

Will keep in touch!

Megan frowned at her phone. It was true, Lily was the last person anyone would suspect of any wrongdoing. She was calm in a crisis, sweet and kind. Megan berated herself for having suggested Lily should pry into Simon's affairs.

She texted Max.

Are you around? Lily was cleaning in the room of one of her guests and saw drugs in a backpack.

It was a few minutes before Max wrote back.

Just on my way to pick up the FBI agent. Is Lily sure it was drugs?

Megan replied.

Well, she wasn't 100% sure but she suspected.

Again, Max took a few minutes to reply.

I'll have to think on that. In theory I could get a search warrant but it's not definite. Tell her to act normal and stay safe.

Done, Megan replied.

Megan was full of anxious energy. Who was this Simon? Why did he have drugs, and did it even matter? Most likely he wasn't the first person to come through Emerson Falls carrying drugs, and he wouldn't be the last. He was just the first person Megan had sent her best friend to spy on. Where had he been headed when he'd broken down? Or had he even broken down? Could a person make their own car break down? And what's more, what kind of drugs were they? White powder … Megan didn't know much about drugs. Cocaine? Heroin? Or maybe it was just powdered sugar and oregano? Maybe Simon was a chef? Maybe they were getting all excited over nothing?

But why did he know Tatum? Had they only met a few days before? She'd seen people work faster than that; it was possible. Maybe they were just two lonely hearts who had found love in an unexpected place?

Megan decided it was time to talk to Jace.

Actors and staff were milling about inside the theater, but the mood was very subdued. Most people looked a little dazed and confused; a few had puffy red eyes from crying. Megan wondered how close these people had been to Bridget. Death had such a strange effect on people, she thought. Even if the person who had died had been a stranger, that death could bring up so many issues and emotions. Fear of their own mortality. Memories of loved ones who had died. Or even simply a breaking point, a crack through which other repressed emotions could come flooding out.

The dim light made it difficult to see but eventually Megan decided Jace wasn't in the main part of the theater. She headed backstage to the office areas, winding past the hallway where she'd seen Bridget with Lester. The memory of the moment flooded her brain and she almost flinched.

The sound of voices coming from the back offices filtered through the air, and Megan followed her ears. She popped her head into a room where two men she didn't know were talking. They stopped talking and stared at her.

"Sorry," Megan said. "I'm looking for Jace?"

One man pointed down the hall. "Check his office," he said, a bit curtly.

"Thanks," Megan murmured, and she continued down the hallway, looking into each doorway. Finally, she found him, alone, sitting at a desk, his elbows on the table, arms propping up his chin. He was either reading something, or staring intently at it. He was motionless; he seemed to be elsewhere.

"Jace," Megan said softly, hoping not to startle him. "I'm Megan Montaigne, the …"

"We've met," Jace said, inhaling deeply and coming out of his trance. He paused, then shrugged. "What can I do for you?" He took off his glasses and rubbed his eyes.

"How are you doing?" Megan asked. The man seemed deflated, like it would take an enormous effort for him to move through the world.

Jace shook his head. "As expected, I suppose?" he said.

Megan nodded. "I'm … well, I'm helping Max. The Deputy. I want to help him figure out what happened here."

"And do we know what happened here?" Jace said abruptly. "Do you know? Because I don't know. No one has told me." He pressed his lips around his teeth.

"I … no, I don't know. What did you see?" Megan said.

Jace inhaled very deeply again and closed his eyes. After a few moments, he looked at Megan and spoke carefully. "The show was over. Most people had gone downstairs to the party. I was up here tying up loose ends, making sure the theater was cleaned up for the night, the audience's trash was picked up, the bathrooms were clear, that sort of thing. There was a prop off on one side of the stage in the wings. Something caught my eye and I saw a foot. I looked, and …" He shook his head.

"It was Bridget," Megan said.

"It was Bridget," Jace repeated.

"Was there any sign of anything?" Megan said. "Like a struggle? I heard she'd vomited. Was there a cup anywhere, a mug? Did she drink something that made her throw up?"

Jace shook his head. "I thought the police were on it? I answered questions already."

"I know," Megan said sympathetically. "I'm just trying to help." She looked around the office. It was sparse. A desk, a chair, a small table with two more chairs. A phone, a lamp, a filing cabinet. She supposed Jace hadn't had time yet to personalize the office, but it was strange, she thought, that there wasn't even a picture of a loved one. On the other hand, she didn't have any pictures of any loved ones on her desk in the library, either. Who was she to judge?

Megan had the feeling Jace wasn't going to put up with her for much longer. She raced through her head, deciding what questions were most important. She wanted to ask him about his relationship with Bridget, and she wanted to ask about Tatum. It seemed more likely that personal questions would lead him to shut down sooner, so she started with the blue-haired girl.

"Tatum says she saw you with Bridget, right after you found her. Do you know why she had stayed behind?" Megan asked.

Jace spread his arms wide, palms up. "Work?" he said. "We couldn't all go straight to the party. She had to do something with the set, I imagine."

Megan nodded. "Do you know … I saw her with a visitor, a guy named Simon. Do you know if she knew him before he came to town?"

Jace looked up almost involuntarily, then looked down again. "Simon?" he said. "She was with a guy after the dress rehearsal. It could have been him, I suppose. I didn't recognize him. Kid with dark hair and a leather jacket."

"That's him," Megan said. "Or at least, that could be him. Did they look like they knew each other?"

Jace smirked. "They looked like they were going to get to know each other pretty well, but I don't know if they knew each other before the show," he said. "Tatum doesn't seem to always make the best choices."

"What do you mean?" Megan asked.

"She needs a lot of attention," Jace said. "People like that don't always make good choices."

"A lot of people make bad choices," Megan said.

"Tatum may not show it when you first meet her, but she craves attention more than she craves anything else," Jace said. "She can't stand when other people get attention she thinks should be hers. Or when other people get attention, period. She would have followed anyone who gave it to her. If this Simon expressed interest, I wouldn't be surprised if they hooked up."

"What about Tatum's interest in you?" Megan wasn't sure there was any actual attraction, but she'd gotten the feeling the other day that there might be. The way Tatum had watched Jace and Bridget together. There had been something more than just general interest in her eyes.

Jace's laugh confirmed Megan's suspicions. "Yes, Tatum seems to be interested in me. Or did. Maybe this Simon will have taken care of that."

"Was Tatum jealous of your relationship with Bridget?" Megan asked.

At this, Jace's eyes shot straight to Megan's. "My relationship with Bridget?" he asked. "What are you suggesting?"

"I'm not suggesting anything," Megan said. "Relationships run the gamut. A bad relationship is still a relationship."

"I did not have a relationship with Bridget," Jace said. "Not the kind you're thinking of."

"I'm not thinking of any kind of relationship," Megan said. "And you did have a relationship with her. You were her boss. That's a relationship."

Jace studied Megan intently. "What are you getting at?" he asked.

"I'm asking whether Tatum might have been jealous of whatever she thought your relationship with Bridget might have been," Megan said. "That's all." She had been right: whatever Jace's relationship with Bridget was, he did not want to discuss it.

"You'll have to ask Tatum," Jace said.

"Do you think Tatum would have been jealous enough to kill?" Megan asked.

Jace subconsciously bared his teeth, then slowly closed his lips again. "I think we're done here," he said.

"Okay," Megan said. "Thanks." She heard Jace stand as she walked out, and he closed the door behind her.

NINETEEN

"Well, that wasn't terribly fruitful," Megan said quietly to the empty hallway. She heard laughter filtering in from the theater area and decided it couldn't hurt to talk to the actors and crew. After all, if there was gossip to be had, a person's co-workers were the most likely to know it. And be talking about it.

The first person Megan saw, aside from the children who were playing tag, was a young woman, maybe early twenties. Megan thought she recognized the girl as the actor who played Liesl. She was seated in the front row, quietly watching what was happening on stage, a somber look on her face, her eyes far away.

"Hi," Megan said, sliding into a seat two away from the woman. "I'm Megan. Library Director," she said, pointing in the direction of the library. "Am I remembering right that you played Liesl?" Megan nodded toward the set.

The young woman smiled slightly, a subdued smile that seemed squashed by something, perhaps the weight of Bridget's death. "Yes," she said. "I'm Abigail."

"Nice to meet you," Megan said. She let a buffer of silence rest

between them for a few minutes, then spoke again. "I'm so sorry about Bridget," she said. Opening a door.

Tears seemed to rush to Abigail's eyes, and she took in a quick
breath. "It's awful," she said. "I can't believe it. I just can't." She
reached into her pocket and pulled out a soft white handkerchief, dabbed carefully at her eyes, then re-folded the cloth and
returned it to its place.

"Were you close?" Megan asked. She still had no idea who
Bridget's friends were. Theater people? Neighbors?

Abigail shook her head. "I don't think Bridget was really close
to anyone," she said. She pulled out the handkerchief and wiped
her eyes again.

"Did you like her, though?" Megan asked. "Was she friendly?
Nice? Kind?"

"Oh, sure," Abigail said. "She was nice enough. Always a little
distant. I heard …" she stopped herself from saying more.

"You heard?" Megan pressed.

"Oh it's gossip," Abigail said. "I shouldn't."

Just as Megan had suspected. Co-workers always knew. Especially in a small town like this one. Megan put her hand on the
seat between them, a way to reach out without invading Abigail's space. "I'm helping the police figure things out," she said.
"It's okay to tell me. I won't think poorly of you."

"Well," said Abigail. "Okay. I heard that Bridget wasn't even
her real name. That she was a *criminal in the protection program.*" The last few words were whispered, slipping off Abigail's
tongue like savory sin.

"Ah," said Megan. Nothing new, after all. "Well, that's partially
true, at least as far as I know. Bridget wasn't her real name. But
I don't know that she was a criminal."

"Oh," said Abigail, a deep blush coloring her cheeks. "I
shouldn't have said anything."

"No, no," said Megan reassuringly. "It's helpful to hear what people are saying. And I don't know everything. Who told you that Bridget was a criminal?"

Abigail shrunk in her seat, clearly embarrassed and uncomfortable. "It's just what people are saying. I don't know who said it. Everyone's talking. It's hard not to overhear."

"It's definitely hard not to overhear," Megan said. "Especially when you're working so closely with others. What else have you heard?"

Abigail shrugged awkwardly. "Well, I mean … it's so awful. I hate to say." She glanced at Megan. "Someone said her father killed her."

"Her *father* killed her?" Megan said carefully. Max had told her to keep an open mind about Lester, but she couldn't convince herself the handsome, quiet man could do such a thing. But she needed to listen to all possibilities. "Tell me more."

"They say her father came from out of town and got into a fight with her and poisoned her drink," Abigail said.

It wasn't impossible, Megan thought. A poisoned drink would fit the crime scene, and Lester likely had opportunity. Anyone did, really, with all the chaos and noise after the show. "Did anyone see her fighting with her father?" Megan asked.

"Well, I don't know," Abigail said. "That's just what they're saying."

"Did they say what the fight was about?" Megan pressed.

"Oh, I suppose over the fact that he left her when she was a baby. That he wasn't around. Someone said they heard …" Abigail glanced at Megan for reassurance that it was okay to continue. Megan nodded. "They heard her mother died from an *overdose*." Again she whispered the last word.

Megan recalled having read that in Bridget's journals, but she wondered how others might have learned that particular tidbit of news. Had someone googled Bridget's name, once they found out her full, real name? Probably, yes, Megan thought. It was human nature. Curiosity was a driving force in humanity. And it was unlikely there would be too many Branwen Heybrooks in the world.

"Do you remember who said her mother died from an overdose?" Megan asked.

"Well, I think it was someone from out of town," Abigail said. "I think it was a woman who seemed to know Lester somehow. Maybe someone staying at Mrs. Bell's place?"

Candace, Megan thought. Why would Candace be talking about Bridget's past? Why, for that matter, would Candace know?

"Did you see the woman?" Megan asked. "Could you describe her?"

"Oh, no," said Abigail. "I didn't hear it directly. It's just … people are talking."

"Yes, of course," Megan said. "Don't worry. You're helping. I know it feels uncomfortable but I really appreciate it. Another question," she said. "Do you think Bridget was … unhappy?"

"Suicidal, you mean?" Abigail said, her face falling with sadness. "I don't know. I didn't know her. She seemed okay?"

"Do you know if she was dating anyone?" Megan asked. "Some people thought she was dating Jace, maybe?"

Abigail blushed again. "I think she liked Jace," Abigail said. "They liked each other."

"What makes you say that?" Megan asked.

"Oh, well, they spent a lot of time together," Abigail said. "They were in his office a lot."

"Did you ever see them acting … you know, intimate? Kissing or anything? Holding hands? Touching?"

Abigail thought a moment. "Well, no. Nothing like that. But they were together a lot."

"Do you think anyone else was jealous of their relationship?" Megan asked.

Abigail's eyes darted around the theater. "Do you mean Tatum?" she whispered.

"Tatum, or anyone," Megan said. Interesting, she thought, that Abigail mentioned Tatum first.

"Tatum seemed to like Jace, and she didn't seem to like the time Bridget spent with him," Abigail said. "But surely she wouldn't …!"

"I know, it's hard to imagine anyone hurting anyone," Megan said. She could feel that Abigail was a sensitive soul, and tried to cushion her words a bit. "Even the worst people have some good in them."

"Yes," said Abigail, nodding fiercely. "That's what I say. Even bad people have people who love them."

"Do you think Tatum is a bad person?" Megan said gently. "Or Jace?"

"Well, no," Abigail said hesitantly. "They're just not quite like me." She looked around to see who might be listening, but everyone else was going about their own business.

"How so?" Megan asked. "How are they different?"

"Well, like Tatum," Abigail said. "A guy came to dress rehearsal, someone she didn't know—that's what I've heard anyway—and next thing I see they're making out up in the balcony. People say … well, that Tatum and the man went out and did … you know, drugs and … stuff, after the show. Intimate stuff. Right after they'd met. That sort of thing. I wouldn't do that." She sniffed slightly. "But I am sure Tatum has many friends who love her."

Megan suppressed a smile. For a person who was trying so hard not to judge, Abigail definitely had opinions.

"How did that guy happen to hook up with Tatum?" Megan said. "How did he pick her out from the crowd?"

"Tatum is … needy," Abigail said. "She'll cling to anyone who will give her attention. Then when they feel suffocated and leave, she becomes moody until the next one comes along. I've only known her for two months and I've seen it a few times already. The guy who plays Rolf," she said, her eyes finding the young man up on the stage. "She was into him for a bit. Ask him."

"I will. Thanks. Regarding the dress rehearsal night again. You said that's when that guy met Tatum. Did you notice anyone else, anyone you didn't know? Anyone who maybe was paying a lot of attention to Bridget?"

Abigail pondered a minute, then brightened. "Yes," she said, pleased at remembering. "An old man. He was keen on her."

"Her father?" said Megan. "I think he was here that night."

"No," said Abigail. "Her father was here too, but this was someone else. An old man who just sat at the back and watched her. She was sitting toward the back, too, with her clipboard and her notes, and he was watching her instead of us."

"Can you describe him?" Megan asked.

"Oh, I don't know. Old. He wasn't really memorable, I guess. He just looked like an old man. Not a local, I know that."

"Did he talk to her at all?" Megan asked, wondering if the old man might have been Giles. "Before or after the show?"

Abagail frowned. "I'm sorry. I didn't notice. I was busy getting notes."

"No, of course, you were doing your job," Megan said. "Back to Jace. Tell me about him. He's new in town. What do you think of him? Do people like him? Is he … I don't know, fair, does he listen, just any impressions you have?"

"He's fine," Abigail said. "He sort of keeps to himself. He's more concerned with the theater than with the show, I think."

"What do you mean?" Megan asked.

"I mean, he didn't really pay attention to the people much." Abigail paused. "Except Bridget."

"Abigail!" A voice from the stage called out, and both Megan and Abigail looked up. It was the director, trying to get the young woman to come join him on stage. He looked a bit frustrated and Abigail immediately rose from her seat, flustered.

"Sorry," Abigail said hastily, and before Megan could reply, Abigail was gone.

Megan thought about what Abigail had said. The fact that she, too, noticed how needy Tatum was interested her, but not as much as the fact that Tatum and Simon—she assumed the person Abigail had seen was Simon—had gone out to do drugs "and stuff." Her mind flipped to worried thoughts for sweet, innocent Lily. No, she thought, Lily was sweet but she was strong and smart, too. She would be fine. Megan hoped.

Megan checked her phone to see if Max had texted her back yet about the search warrant, or anything else, but she had no new messages. Off picking up the new FBI agent, who might well take away the diaries.

"Back to Bridget's journals," Megan said. "Please let there be clues."

TWENTY

It's so easy to slip up.

You slip up in ways you don't even think about.

Like water. I mean water, it's simple, right? There's water everywhere. Obviously.

But Emerson Falls compared to Tucson, it's ridiculous.

In Tucson, there are lakes. Water exists.

In Emerson Falls, the whole town identity is water. Literally. There are the falls, Emerson Falls, and then there's the Skagit River. When you're near either of them, the sound of the water is incessant. You get used to it, sure. It's white noise. Background music.

But there's no silence like desert silence.

Emerson Falls can never be quiet like that. It's too full of life.

I almost said something to someone the other day. Just a random comment at the grocery store. About how the sound of the water never goes away. About how it's not like that in Arizona. Would that have been so wrong? Would that have blown my cover? I'm not the only person in the world who has been to Arizona.

I look at these people and they all seem so pure. Being around Joel's friends for so long, I'm used to a rawness. Hard core. Here they all have their shiny veneers on. You just know at least some of them are faking it. You know that at least some of them have dirty laundry, closets filled with skeletons. Secrets they will take with them to the grave.

I'm not used to everything being hidden like that. Facades.

Back home, you knew what was what. Here, everyone's trying to pretend they've got it all figured out.

It's almost enough to drive me to drugs. Something to take the edge off.

I won't. I've thought about it. But I'm going to do better than my mom.

I'm going to live forever.

Joel did drugs sometimes. Not a lot. Especially considering his job. Some weed, some coke, some smack. A friend kept trying to get him to use something he was trying to get people hooked on … propofol, I think. It's not regulated, so it's easy to steal. If you do it right it knocks you unconscious and then you wake up euphoric a few minutes later. Giddy. A brief escape from reality, but it doesn't last.

That's the only drug I ever did. Propofol.

I did it just for Joel. He wanted me to try. Just the once.

It knocked me out and then when it wore off it scared me. There's a fine line with propofol between being high and being dead. They use it sometimes for lethal injections. Death penalty. Using it for fun is playing with fire.

Overdose would be so easy. After it wore off, I was terrified. I saw myself following my mother down the hole. Down to hell.

That's when I started trying to get Joel to leave it all. Walk away.

I guess that's the beginning of how he died.

How I got him killed.

It's weird. Those people, yeah they're messed up, but they're humans. They were the closest thing I had to friends.

I wonder if anyone down there misses me.

Joel thought they all loved me but I don't know. I don't know if they knew what love was.

"You're the kind of woman that guys are afraid to get close to," he told me. "And then when you're gone, when you finally decide you deserve better and you move on, you're all they think about. That's the kind of woman you are."

He always called me a woman, not a girl. Nineteen and barely able to vote but I wasn't just a girl to him. "You see who people are," he said. "You pay attention. People who hate themselves don't want to be near people who really see them. But then when you're gone, they miss it. They miss being known."

I didn't believe him. It's always been so hard for me to get close to people. It feels like they all push me away, keep me at arm's length.

"If that's true," I said to him, "there must be a lot of people who hate themselves in the world."

He laughed. "Yes. Thus, the drugs."

"You see me," I said.

"Because I've been looking for you," he said.

Megan looked at the date on the journal entry: nearly three years prior. She recalled Betty and Carol saying that Bridget had moved in about three and a half years ago, so this must have been right after she had moved to Emerson Falls. Megan did some quick math in her head and decided Bridget must have been about twenty-four when she died, maybe twenty-five.

Far too young.

Megan flipped forward a few pages. There were five notebooks, and she had only made it about halfway through the first. If the FBI agent was going to take them away, Megan wanted to read as much as she could first.

She checked the time: four o'clock. The show down at the theater would begin at seven, and Megan wanted to be there early.

She read on.

I got a job, working at a nearby hotel. Housekeeping. Sort of risky in a way, in that anyone randomly coming to the hotel could see me. On the other hand, housekeeping staff seem to be invisible to most people, so I'm guessing no one will notice me. Pay is okay, not great, but jobs are hard to find for someone with my skill levels. I need to ask the marshals about education. Maybe I could go to school or something but how do I even do that if I'm pretending not to be who I am? Do I need to show my high school diploma? Can they fake a new diploma for me? Probably they can. If they can get me a new birth certificate, they can get me a new diploma.

I haven't made any friends yet. I'm not naturally outgoing and I'm scared of everyone. What would I talk about? Where I grew up? My family?

I always liked acting. Maybe I just need to create a whole new character for myself. Who is Bridget Hill? What's her back story? What's her motivation?

I think she should be a good chef. I've always wanted to be a better cook. Maybe in this life I am. So Bridget Hill, organized, creative, good chef. Likes birds and big cats. Very patient. Good listener. Ugh, that's all boring. What else. Skydiving. Maybe she's a skydiver. I could do that. Why not? What do I have to lose? And what about Bridget's family? It's probably easiest to say I was an orphan. Is that even a thing anymore? Are there still orphanages? I need to find out. Either way, my parents will have to be out of the picture. Not that that's a stretch. And no siblings. Also not a stretch, though who knows how many half siblings I might have.

I wonder. I wonder if one day I could meet all my half siblings. Maybe they'll have a gathering and I'll show up as the caterer and I'll listen in. Maybe one of them would prove trustworthy enough that I could tell him or her my secret. Maybe then I could have family again.

Is it even possible to make a real connection to other people ever again?

Am I going to be forever alone?

Megan's heart ached reading this. She wondered the same thing. Certainly no one in town had had a clue about Bridget's real identity. And, she thought, as far as she knew, no one in town had really gotten close to her.

Or had they? A thought of Jace flew to Megan's mind. What had their relationship been? Had he simply been the boss? Why had he taken such an interest in Bridget, when he apparently hadn't been interested in anyone else? He'd shown up out of nowhere to manage the theater. What was his past?

Megan googled his name but came up empty. That wasn't a surprise; some people managed to stay out of online searches better than others. Max, for example. She could never find any real good scoop on Max.

"I should have Max over more often," Megan said to the journals. She liked him. She'd missed her opportunity to invite Bridget up. Life was short and unpredictable. Megan decided she needed to make more of an effort with the people she cared about.

"Just a friendly thing," she said to the journals. "Not a date."

She returned to the journals, flipping farther ahead.

I know it would be best if I just forgot all about my old life.

Knowing I still have to testify, and knowing those people want me dead, makes that hard.

I need some hobbies. Maybe Bridget Hill is a hiker. Long walks just mean a lot of time for the brain to wander, though. I need to find a hobby that uses my mind. Robot building or something. But not robot building.

I'm just back from the library. I made a fake email account and a fake Facebook page there. I'll only use it from the library, not from my own house. I don't think they can track me? I don't know how that works.

I spent an hour looking through the pages of people I knew in Tucson. Joel's friends, their girlfriends, anyone I could find. The guys don't post much but a lot of their girlfriends have their pages public, whether they realize it or not. I saw one talking about me. Her boyfriend is one of the top guys and he's pissed because they'd trusted Joel so much. I mean, Joel was a trust-worthy guy. Of course they trusted him. I'm the one who pulled him away. The girlfriend is saying she knew all along that I was trouble. She said she could see it in my eyes. My eyes looked too judgmental, she said. Superior. Like I thought I was better than all of them.

She said if she saw me she'd shoot me between my judgmental eyes, just because it would make her happy to knock that look off my face.

Megan took a deep breath and closed the notebook. She couldn't imagine reading that about herself. What a life Bridget had had in Emerson Falls. And what a death.

"I'm going to find who did it, Bridget," she said softly. "I will."

TWENTY-ONE

Candace and Giles were sitting in the lounge at the B&B enjoying afternoon tea and the delicious, delicate sandwiches, cookies, and savory treats Lily had set out for her guests. Candace was feeling particularly euphoric, having given herself a small hit of propofol about half an hour prior. At first she'd been worried, with Giles retiring, that she wouldn't be able to get access to it anymore. But Candace knew no one could reject her charms. She'd cunningly befriended a few of the staff, and she was no longer concerned about running out. She sold most of it. Gave her a little extra spending money for expenses she didn't want to have to explain to Giles.

Giles, for his part, was sitting in an overstuffed chair, staring out the window. Moping, Candace thought.

Not for the first time, Candace did some mental calculations around their ages. Hers and Giles's. He was sixty-five. She was forty-seven. Forty-seven wasn't old but it was almost fifty, and the lines were starting to show on her face. And her hands. The hands were the worst. If she was going to find the love of her life, or at least someone to take care of her for the second half, she would have to do it soon before she looked too old to catch anyone worthwhile. Reflexively she reached up to touch her forehead, imagining it as if looking in a mirror. The lines between her eyebrows were the worst. Too much frowning. Glowering, Giles would call it. He said she glowered. At first she thought he meant "glowed," but then she said it to someone else and they set her straight.

Candace tried relaxing her forehead and thought again about botox. Her friend Maryanne did botox once and ended up looking like she'd had a stroke. Candace wasn't sure it was worth the risk, but she was tempted. Maybe a boob lift would be in order. Giles wouldn't mind. Then again he might not notice.

What Candace had noticed was that Giles had noticed Lester's daughter. The previous night at the show. He'd made Candace wait around in the theater after the show was over. She'd thought he'd wanted to meet the actors. Maria, maybe; Maria was portrayed by a very pure-looking woman in her early thirties. Smooth skin and a clear, innocent smile and perfectly straight teeth, though if anyone had asked Candace she would have said Maria's eyes looked like there was nothing behind them but a blank mind. No one had asked Candace, though. Or perhaps Giles would have wanted to meet the Captain. That actor seemed quite bright. He was handsome and fit and oozed charm. Unlike Maria's eyes, his eyes danced in a way that told you there was something going on upstairs. Candace might have liked to talk to him herself, but he was an actor and undoubtedly poor.

But no, when the theater had started to clear, it was Lester's daughter that Giles sought out. He'd called her Bridget, so either he didn't know yet that she was really Branwen or he was playing along with the scam. It was obvious they'd met before. Candace had rolled her eyes and gone downstairs to the party. When she'd come upstairs a bit later to retrieve the jacket she'd left on the back of her seat, Giles was gone. She'd found him again downstairs, but he'd been distracted and inattentive. Which, of course, was normal these days.

Candace looked at her husband now, still staring out the window. She reminded herself that she did not yet have his money and it wouldn't do for him to leave her for someone younger. She took a few moments to try to erase the frown that she could tell had crept back to her forehead.

"Darling," she said. "Did you try these cucumber sandwiches? I don't even know how a person can slice the cucumbers so thin. They're perfect. Try one."

Giles blinked himself back into the room and gave a grunt as the fog of his thoughts cleared.

"Hmmm," he said.

Candace watched as he walked to the table, prepared a plate for himself full of the various sandwiches and treats, and shuffled back to his chair by the window. Objectively, he wasn't an unattractive man. He was still fit, and if she turned off the part of her mind that was annoyed by his very breathing, she knew he could be as charming and interesting as the actor who played the Captain had seemed to be. She didn't share his fascination with birds, but she'd spent so much time at the travel agency in Tucson directing birders to the best birding sites that she at least knew the language. It had been years since she'd worked that job, but without even thinking she could rattle off all the best spots. Buenas Aires National Wildlife Refuge, Madera Canyon, Sabino Canyon, Sweetwater Wetlands Park. The Chiracahua Mountains, the Huachuca Mountains, Ramsey Canyon Preserve. San Pedro Riparian National Conservation Area and the Patagonia-Sonoita Preserve. And more. People didn't think of Arizona as a place for birding, but the birders knew. One of the top ten places in North America for birding, she'd told many a birder. Five hundred and fifty species. Come visit us.

For whatever reason, birding seemed to attract more men than women. At least, that's how it seemed to Candace. Her theory was that women were tasked with actually raising children and taking care of households and making the world go around. Men could take off on a whim and know, without asking, that women would pick up the slack, as women always did. A woman who wanted to chase birds for a week or a month or a year would have to find someone to cover for every chore she was responsible for. Feeding the kids. Taking care of the parents. Keeping the home light lit for the husband, whenever he decided to return. Men had time to go off for a year checking birds off a list, and they did it without a thought for who or what they left behind. Women had to hold up the world.

Candace sighed with bitterness.

Giles looked up and Candace re-pasted a smile on her face. If only she'd been born independently wealthy. If only she'd decided to become an anesthesiologist instead of marrying one.

"Well hello, folks!" A deep, gravely voice filled the room, breaking the silence that had permeated and chilled the air between Candace and Giles. Candace looked up to see the young man who had arrived about the same time they had. Simon.

"Hello, Simon," Candace said. She looked him up and down, assessing. The clothes he was wearing were borrowed from Lily, she knew, so she couldn't really judge him on that. Lily had good enough taste. Simon was neither handsome nor unattractive. He looked a bit fidgety, like he had trouble sitting still. His eyes, Candace noticed, didn't sit in front of a blank mind but rather a brick wall. There was much going on in his head, but his eyes would reveal none of it. Also, they were a bit red.

"Crazy about last night, eh?" Simon said. Noisily, he grabbed a plate and filled it to overflowing with the dainty foods. He picked up a cucumber sandwich, inspected the insides like vegetables had never occurred to him, shrugged, and took a bite. "Not bad," he said, stuffing the rest of the small sandwich in his mouth.

"Would you like some tea?" Candace offered, pointing to the hot water and the tray with an array of flavors.

"Do they got coffee?" Simon said through another mouthful of sandwich.

Candace poured him some coffee and handed it to him. She wondered how many times in her life she had poured coffee for men who were perfectly capable of lifting a pot and pouring it for themselves. Everything we do for show, she thought. Everything we do to make men happy.

"So did they figure out how that girl died?" Simon said casually. He looked at Giles, staring out the window.

"I haven't heard much," Candace said. "I've heard maybe overdose of something. Her mother was an addict."

"Oh?" said Simon, somewhat disinterestedly. "You knew her?" He looked over at Giles again.

Candace followed his gaze and internally rolled her eyes. Did Giles pay attention to anything anymore? Well, he'd seemed to be interested in Bridget. What had they talked about? Had he known who she was?

"Her father is Lester Heybrook. He's staying here too," Candace said.

"Yeah, I heard that," Simon said, examining a miniature quiche. "The good-looking old guy. You know him, then?"

From his seat by the window Giles laughed, startling Candace. "Oh, she knew him," Giles said. "More than once, I'd say." The food was still sitting, mostly untouched, on his plate. He picked up a shortbread cookie and nibbled at the edge.

Simon raised his eyebrows at Candace. "That true?" he said. "You and the old guy?" He made a gesture that Candace thought was a bit rude.

"Long before Giles," Candace said, trying to keep the edge out of her voice.

"They go way back," Giles said. He didn't turn from the window. Candace wondered if he was watching something out there, or just watching his thoughts float by.

"So the girl could be your daughter?" Simon winked several times at Candace, cackling.

"The girl was *not* my daughter," Candace said. Her euphoria was wearing off. It was obvious Simon knew he was stirring up trouble. No, Lester hadn't stuck around long enough for Candace to have any children with him. She, like every other woman, had been all but helpless against his unwitting charms. Back then, as perhaps still now, he'd been oblivious to the effect he had on the female of the species, and a few of the males. When he'd settled with any woman for any length of time it always seemed he'd done it out of a sense of obligation. Like it was what he was supposed to do more than what he wanted. Candace had been sure she could be the one to tame him, but all she'd gotten were a few intermittent months. She'd always suspected it was because she had a young child at the time. Her son. In one sense, Lester had been so detached that it seemed it didn't even matter. Candace had always thought that if Lester had stayed around, been a father figure, her son wouldn't have gotten into so much trouble. Might have run with a different group, one that wasn't always in and out of prison. Her son might even have become a birder himself. Not that she would wish that on anyone, but it might have been better, all things considered.

By the time Giles came around, Candace's son was out of the house. He didn't exert any fatherly influence, and had never really tried to form a bond with him.

In a sense, everything that had ever gone wrong in Candace's life was either Giles's fault, or Lester's. Or so it seemed from her perspective.

"Going to the show tonight?" Simon said, grabbing another quiche and stuffing the whole thing in his mouth at once. He wiped his fingers on a tiny napkin and then reached for a petit four.

"We thought we might," Candace said, looking at her husband. "To show solidarity to the cast and crew. Are you going?"

"Wouldn't miss it," Simon said, winking again. "There's a cute number with blue hair workin' there. Thought I'd get a refill tonight."

Candace blanched internally at the crude suggestion but kept her face serene. Did men even realize how offensive their comments were sometimes? But something about this man told her it was best not to get on his bad side. And from experience she knew how easy it would be to get on the bad side of a man like this. "Hopefully you'll have a lovely night," she said.

"That'd be one way to describe it," Simon cackled. He winked at Giles, who wasn't paying attention.

"How long are you here?" Candace asked the young man, watching as he devoured yet another quiche.

Simon shrugged. "Car should be done Monday. I'll be out of here as soon as I can. Nothing to keep me here."

"Not even the lovely blue-haired girl?" said Candace.

"Nah," he laughed. "I gave it my best but she's just not the one." He filled a napkin with several more sandwiches and quiches. "I'll see you all at the theater," he said as he trotted out of the room.

"We will see you there," said Candace to the space where he'd been. Giles said nothing at all.

TWENTY-TWO

Megan sat on her balcony, laptop warming her lap. Remnants of her black bean and quinoa salad dotted the bowl on the table next to her, and her glass of red wine was almost empty. Megan was leaning to the side of the chair, her head propped up by her left arm as she scrolled through a browser window with her right.

She was searching the internet, trying to find out more about the various people in town who seemed suspect to her. After some deep digging she'd managed to find Candace's maiden name, and now she was looking through anything she could find on Candace Turner Levine. The fact that there were multitudes of Candace Turners made it all the more difficult. She was never sure whether she was looking at the right one.

"Candace Turner ... Arizona ..." Megan said to the screen. She squinted. "... children." She typed the keywords into the search bar and hit enter, but all that came up was articles about children's agencies and a man with the last name of Turner who had been shot.

"Ugh!" Megan said. "These companies can track every move I make but they can't figure out which Candace Turner I'm trying to find?"

She exhaled deeply and tried again.

Giles Levine she typed into the search bar, then added *Arizona*. Remembering that Lily had told her Giles's profession, she added *anesthesiologist*.

This time she had more luck. A Giles Levine was listed in a directory of anesthesiologists for Tucson. Megan clicked on the link and learned that Giles had been board certified and a former Director of Anesthesia. In his off time, the site told Megan, Giles enjoyed spending time with his wife, birding, and golf.

"I'm not saying that's a bio to put a person to sleep, but if I were a comedian I might." Megan grinned and nodded her head with amusement at her anesthesiology joke. She looked around. If only the woodland creatures could have enjoyed that joke as much as she had, she thought.

"All right, then," she said. "Simon."

She texted Lily.

What is Simon's last name? I know he told us but I forgot.

Quickly the three dots appeared, followed by a text from Lily.

Nash

Megan replied:

Has he seemed to notice you were in his room?

Not yet, Lily wrote. *All good so far!*

Megan sighed with relief.

Simon Nash she typed into the search bar, but even as she did she knew it would be futile. When she saw "about 100,000,000 results" appear at the top of the search page, she shook her head. She poked through the entries for Simon Nash on LinkedIn, but gave up after a few dozen.

"The people I want to investigate should be required to have unique names," Megan said to the search results.

Finally she typed in *Branwen Heybrook*.

Here, the results were much more fruitful. Sparse, but the few results Megan found seemed all to be for the right person. Most of the results were brief mentions in articles about the death of Joel, who turned out to be Joel Bowman. Joel, the articles said, had been part of a large drug conspiracy centered in Tucson, Arizona, for eight years. He was killed, police assume, by members of the conspiracy. Branwen Heybrook, the victim's girlfriend, is believed to have been a witness to the death and possible informant. Ms. Heybrook has not been reached for comment.

Tucson, Megan thought. A lot of roads lead back to Tucson. Not just Branwen, but Candace and Giles as well. And, probably, Lester. Coincidence? Or did it all mean something?

Megan searched finally for a phone number for A-A-Art's Collision Repair. The phone rang eight times before someone answered.

"A-A-Art's," a woman said curtly.

"Hi, this is Megan Montaigne from Emerson Falls," Megan said. "I'm working … well, I can't say much but I'm helping the police on something and I'm wondering if you or someone can answer some questions."

"You're police?" the woman said.

"Well, I'm a police consultant," Megan said. It was true. Just because she had been hired to read journals didn't mean she wasn't a consultant.

"What do you need?" the woman asked.

"I'm wondering about a car you have in the shop there," Megan said. "From a Simon Nash."

The woman paused. "I can't tell you about someone else's business," she said.

"No, I get that," Megan said. "It's for the police." She bit her lip, hoping the woman wouldn't challenge her again.

The woman paused again. "Hang on," she said, and ragged

hold music assaulted Megan's ears for a few minutes.

When the hold music stopped, a new person was on the line.

"Hello?" said a man with a deep, rough voice.

"Hello," said Megan. "I'm Megan Montaigne, from Emerson Falls. I'm working with the police—"

"Yeah, I heard that. What do you want?" the man said.

"Well, you have a car there from a man named Simon Nash," Megan said.

"Yeah?" the man said, his tone saying, *yes, I do, what do you want with it?*

"I'm wondering, the damage to the car … is it something … well, is it something someone could have done to their own car?"

The man on the other end was breathing heavily, as though he'd been running, but Megan thought maybe he was just a heavy breather. "Did he bust his own car? That's what you want to know?" The man clearly thought Megan was insane.

"I'm not asking if he *did*," Megan said. "I'm just wondering, the damage that has been done, is it something he *could* have caused himself?"

Megan could almost hear the man shrugging.

"Look, lady, I mean I guess he could have? Why would he do that? That would be an asinine move," the man said.

"Yes, I get that," Megan said. This man did not read enough mystery books or watch enough crime TV, she thought. Where was his imagination? "I'm just wondering if it's possible."

She pictured the man shrugging and shaking his head this time.

"Sure, he could have. Could have stuck a big chunk of metal on the road and then run into it full speed. But who would do that?" the man asked.

"Someone who needed a reason to get stuck in a town for a few days," Megan said. "Okay, thank you, sir. I appreciate your—"

The man hung up.

"Good talking to you, too," Megan said to the phone.

She sighed heavily. It was now six o'clock. The next showing of *The Sound of Music* downstairs was scheduled to begin at seven. Megan had been planning to go, to see if she could stir up some clues, but she just couldn't bear the thought of it right now.

On a whim, she texted Max.

Are you going to the show tonight? Sound of Music? she wrote.

A few minutes later Max replied.

Just got Agent Silva settled. He doesn't really seem interested in my help. I hadn't decided on the show. Why?

Want to go to Bezauberung instead? There's live music and dancing there tonight, Megan wrote.

The pause before Max's reply was longer this time. Was he talking with Agent Silva? Or was he trying to figure out how to let Megan down easy?

Yes, Max finally wrote. *That would be fun. I'm off duty tonight. I can have a drink, even.*

Megan felt a flitter of joy.

Pick me up at seven? she wrote.

I'll be there :), Max wrote.

"A smiley face!" Megan said, her own face echoing the text. "I got a smiley face out of Deputy Max Coleman! My, my." Megan rushed to her closet. "What to wear? What to wear?" Flipping through the hangers, she grazed her fingers over each piece. "Not you, not you, not you …" she said to the clothes until finally picking out a black top with a deep-cut back, her favorite jeans, and low black pumps.

"This is not a date," she told the shoes. "Not a date."

TWENTY-THREE

Max arrived at two minutes before seven, pleasing Megan's punctual heart.

"You look nice," he said appreciatively as she stepped into his car.

"Why thank you, sir," Megan said. "You do, too. I hardly ever see you out of uniform." Max was wearing brown chinos with a close-fitting long-sleeved white Henley shirt and suede desert boots. Megan raised an eyebrow in approval. Max smiled.

As they drove away from the library, Megan noted the parking lot was packed with people attending the show. "I can't believe they didn't cancel," she said. "What a mood they'll have in there tonight."

"I suppose it would be a lot of hassle to refund all the tickets," Max said. "That saying, 'the show must go on,' I guess it's not just a cliché." He turned his car out of Emerson Falls and headed west on the highway toward the restaurant.

"How Lester must be feeling," Megan said. "I should check on him. It doesn't seem like he has a lot of people." She couldn't imagine how lonely his life must have been. Or Bridget's, for that matter. But maybe they liked it like that. Still, everyone needed people. Again she felt a twinge of guilt over not having reached out to the young woman. "I should have been a better neighbor," she said out loud.

"You're thinking of Bridget?" Max said.

Megan nodded.

"It's not your fault. You're a busy person. You can't take care of everyone," he said.

"I know, but it made me think about how often we just assume there will be more time," Megan said. "Like, we assume that every day, all day long. There could be an earthquake right now that split the road open and we could fall in and that'd be the last of us."

Max laughed, the guffaw Megan loved so much. "As earthquake-prone as this region is, I seriously doubt we'd be sucked into a gaping hole in the earth. And if we were, I'd save you."

Megan smiled at him. "Thanks, Max. You're the best. And I'll hold you to that."

They arrived at the restaurant and were seated immediately. The tables were made of thick, rustic, dark wood, with chairs to match; strands of twinkly lights were wound around equally dark floor-to-ceiling posts, giving the space a magical atmosphere.

"Max!" Megan whispered. "Look! Owen is here!" She pointed at a table in the corner where her assistant was seated with another man. Owen was laughing and glowing, and the other man was staring at Owen with a look of adoration.

"That must be the mysterious No," Max said, his voice filled with delight. "Should we …?"

"No," said Megan. "Not yet. We'll keep an eye on them and say hello before they leave." She felt her grin beaming on her face, ear to ear. Seeing Owen so happy warmed her heart.

A waiter came over and served them some bread and cheese. "Katenbrot, or 'barn bread,' and some Gouda. Would you care for anything to drink?" she said.

Max looked at Megan and indicated she should order first.

"I'll have the Bee Killer," Megan said, pointing at the menu to the drink made with the German liqueurs Killepitsch and Bärenjäger.

"Is that good?" Max asked her. "Have you had it?"

"Delicious," Megan said. "I've had it here a couple of times. The Pink Honey Martini is good, too, but tonight I'm up for a bit of a sting."

Max looked at the waiter. "I'll have the same."

The waiter left to fill their orders, and Max dug into the bread.

"So," Megan said. "Agent Silva. What do you think?"

Max shook his head. "I am definitely getting the vibe that Agent Silva definitely doesn't really want my help on this case," he said.

"You mentioned that," Megan said. "What gives you that feeling?"

Max finished chewing, thinking a bit about his answer. "He's very … terse. Not particularly forthcoming with either questions or answers. Won't tell me anything about what he knows about Bridget's, or rather Branwen's … I guess participation in the witness protection program. Participation seems like a weird word. Her time served maybe. Seems a bit like a jail sentence, if you ask me." He chewed on another bite of bread, the look on his face telling Megan his mind was still whirling on his thoughts. "There's a lot he isn't telling me, and I have no way to find out what it is. I hate that," he said.

"Would he have access to all the information?" Megan asked. "I tried to find some information about the program, but it's all a closely held secret. I want to call the U.S. Marshals' office and see if they'll tell me anything, but of course, it's the weekend."

Max shook his head. "I doubt they'd tell you anything anyway. The system only works because no one knows anything. For all we know, there could be ten other people in Emerson Falls in the program. You, for example," his eyes twinkled, "could be in the program, and I'd never know."

Megan laughed. "You caught me! I am not really Megan Montaigne. I'm Emmalina Potts, Marchioness of Katenbrot. I had to leave my home and everything I loved when I saw the Baroness of Beekillerville in intimate liaison with the Duke of Bärenjäger, much to the dismay of the Duchess of Bärenjäger. The Duke threatened to have me killed to keep it all quiet. It was quite a scene. But I feel safe now in Emerson Falls, thanks largely to the local coppers, who are strong and dashing and wise."

Max was laughing and shaking his head through Megan's description. "You just came up with all that?" he said with admiration.

"I did," Megan said. "I mean, no, I didn't make it up. It's all true. You can call me Emmalina now. Or Marchioness, if you'd rather."

"What exactly is a Marchioness?" Max said. "That's a new one to me. Is that a real thing?"

"Oh yes," said Megan. "Lower in the ranks than the Duchess, higher than the Countess. Certainly higher than the Baroness of Beekillerville." Megan tipped her nose into the air. She then softened. "I can't even imagine having to give up my whole life and start over with nothing. Not only leaving friends and family but having that option completely taken away from me. Do you think you could do it?"

"I don't know," Max said. "In some ways, in my line of work, I see how people are pretending to be someone else all the time. Maybe it would be easier for some to start from scratch. Get a second chance."

The waiter came back to take their orders. When she was gone, they continued their conversation.

"Who would you be if you had a second chance?" Megan asked. "What would you change?"

Max twirled his fork between his fingers. "I'm pretty happy with my life, honestly," he said. "Right now, I can't think of anything I'd want to change."

Megan sighed. "That's just the thing, though, isn't it? Before her boyfriend was killed, Bridget—Branwen—may have been perfectly happy with her life, too, and then suddenly it was all taken away from her. She decided to love someone, and loving him … I mean it destroyed her life. That's a high price."

"Is it a price you'd pay?" Max asked.

Megan looked at Max, his face glowing in the dim room, lit by the twinkly lights and a few candles on the table. His smile, his dark eyes, those perfect teeth, it all had a different look tonight. Like a landscape she'd seen a million times under the bright summer sun, but was now for the first time seeing by moonlight.

"I've paid a pretty high price for love before," Megan said.

Max leaned back, his eyebrows drawn together. "I'm sorry. I forgot. You were engaged."

Megan nodded. Her fiancé, Zeus, had died a few years before in a plane crash. She had moved on, in some ways, but she did wonder if her heart would ever come out fully again from behind the wall she'd built around it.

"It's okay," Megan said. "But I wonder about Bridget. Anyone in that program. How could you ever get close to anyone if you couldn't tell them your life story? Everything would be a lie. Are you who you are if no one else can ever see you? It seems like it would be unbearable. I mean, for me, what I want in a relationship, what I want is for someone to truly know me. Not just to be willing to listen to me when I talk, but to crave knowledge of me. To want to know not just what I think or feel but to want to know why. To want to explore my heart and mind. And I want to feel the same about him. Branwen, once she became Bridget, could never really have that again. How would she answer if someone wanted to know her better? Questions like, Who are you? What do you think about when you can't sleep? Why do you love the things you love? What are your secrets? I mean, how could she answer? What could she say?"

Max nodded, looking down at the fork in his fingers, then he looked back at Megan, holding her eyes. "Marchioness Emmalina, tell me: Who are you? What do you think about when you can't sleep? Why do you love the things you love? What are your secrets?"

Megan's mouth opened but her mind went blank. What was he getting at? What did he want?

"Hey, you two!" While Max and Megan had been lost in conversation, Owen and his companion had finished dinner and now stood at their table. Owen had a distinctly mischievous look on his face as he glanced from Megan to Max and back. Ever so slightly he raised an eyebrow in Megan's direction, and she felt herself blush.

"Owen!" Megan said brightly, perhaps too brightly. "We saw you guys and were going to come over in a bit before you left!"

"We're leaving now," Owen said. "Thought we'd say hi on the way out." He turned to the man next to him. With Owen's hair, the two were about the same height; if Owen had been bald, the other man would have been an inch or two taller. He was lean with good posture; his light blond hair was cut short and his smile was bright and friendly. "This is Parker," Owen said. "Megan, Max."

Max stood to shake hands with Parker. "Nice to meet you, Parker," he said, his grin a bit wider than normal. "Any friend of

Owen is a friend of mine."

"Max is a police officer," Owen said to Parker, "so watch your P's and Q's."

Parker smiled. "Will do. Nice to meet you, Max." He reached for Megan's outstretched hand. "Megan. Owen has told me all about you."

"Even the bad stuff is true, probably," Megan said. "Owen is a very good judge of character. I'm so glad to meet you. But you can't leave now. The music and dancing are about to start!" Up on the stage, the musicians were just getting set, checking their instruments and the microphones and pointing at speakers as they talked to someone on staff.

"That is *exactly* why we're leaving now," Owen said. "I do not dance. We'll see you guys later," he said. He turned slightly so Max couldn't see his face, and gave Megan a wink.

"Nice meeting you," Parker said. As they turned, he put a protective hand to Owen's back.

"Aww," said Megan, watching them go. "No seems nice."

"He does," Max said. "Good for Owen."

"So what about you, Max?" Megan said. "Will you dance?" The music was just starting, and a few brave souls had rushed to the dance floor.

"I will dance badly," Max said. "But I will absolutely dance."

Their food arrived just then, and they ate and talked enthusiastically until finally Max stood, put out his hand to Megan, and led her to the dance floor, where they laughed abundantly and danced badly until the band went home.

TWENTY-FOUR

I didn't really want to be alive when I got here. I also didn't want to be dead, but it didn't feel like there was much difference.

A few weeks ago it got to a boiling point.

I was ready to give up.

The drudgery and hopelessness of every day was dark and unbearable. No friends. No one to turn to. Nothing I could say even if someone were there.

I couldn't see the point of going on. I was clinging to a past that I couldn't bring back. I had nothing else. No future. No self.

Then one night the weight of it all came crashing down on me so heavily in a terrible, frightening nightmare. I was in a black hole and I couldn't escape. I could see out, but no one could see in. No one could help me.

I woke up at two in the morning. Sweating. My heart was racing and I felt sick. I was certain I was about to die.

In what I thought were my final moments, I realized how desperately I wanted to live.

I made it through the night, sleeping with the light on. In the morning I went for a walk to Addie's Park, and I sat there and talked with her ghost, out loud, for what must have been hours.

Did she reply? In her way, she did.

She reminded me how young she was when she died.

How much life she missed out on.

She told me that if she could live again, even if it meant giving up everything she'd ever have, she wouldn't think for even a moment. She would take the opportunity in a heartbeat.

As many heartbeats as she could have. She would take them.

To be able to sit in the sun by the river again.

To feel the spray of the falls on her face.

To take in a breath of this sweet Emerson Falls air.

One more hour, one more day. She would take it.

And here I am with not just an hour or a day, but the rest of my life.

This is my life now. It's a reboot, not a death sentence.

People talk all the time about what they would do with a second chance.

And here I have one.

All the things I did that hurt people.

All the things I said that I regretted the moment they were out of my mouth.

All the wrong turns, all the mistakes.

It's like a reincarnation where I don't have to forget everything I ever learned.

The mistakes were paved over. No one will ever know. And I get to stay. Alive.

I get to start over from scratch. To be whoever I want to be. My best self.

I don't want to spend every day just hiding from death, from the people who want me dead. I want to live each day so fully that if I were to die tomorrow, I'd have no regrets.

My goal is no longer simply to avoid death. My goal now is to *live*.

Three, almost three and a half years later, and ...

No, it's not love. Not yet.

Three, almost three and a half years later and I'm dating again. Love can wait a while.

I rushed it last time. I learned my lesson.

I'm terrified.

I'm exhilarated.

A couple of weeks ago I went to the hotel to pick up my last paycheck, now that I have the job at the new theater by the library.

Sitting in the office was a guy I hadn't met before. New manager. Crisp white shirt. Burgundy tie with tiny white polka dots. Short, mousy brown hair with a cowlick that looked like it had a mind of its own.

How unfair that men can have mousy brown hair and cowlicks without being judged.

I knocked on the door frame. He looked up.

"You're Bridget," he said. His eyes, river blue. Running deep.

I'd called and told them I was coming in, so he must have known. But he said my name like it was an answer to a bigger question neither of us had asked but we both needed to know. Like he was reading my future. Or his.

"It's a good thing you're not my boss," I said as he handed over my paycheck. He held my eyes and held onto the check a little too long. Like we were holding hands, not holding two ends of the same envelope.

"Oh?" he said, finally letting go.

"Yes," I said. "That means it's okay for you to ask me out."

I guess in that moment my brain decided I was done with being alone.

I watched a movie the other night, *Into the Wild*. The next day I went to the library and got the book it was based on, and I read it straight through. It's a reenactment or recreation, I guess. Not a true story, really, as the guy it's based on died. But the author recreated his interpretation of events, as best as he could follow it. It's about a guy who was tired of our modern materialistic world, so he went off into the wilderness of Alaska, by himself, to find himself.

Instead, he got lost, got sick, and died.

The line that struck me the most was something the guy wrote in a book, not too long before he died. Alone, weak, hungry, lost in the Alaskan wilderness, probably knowing he'd never see another person again in his life, he wrote: "Happiness only real when shared."

Happiness only real when shared.

I feel alive again.

I feel renewed.

I've decided to live. And deciding to live means deciding to love.

I may have a past I can't talk about. But I am not alone, weak, hungry, nor lost in the Alaskan wilderness. I'm in Emerson Falls, one of the most beautiful places in the world, with loads of fine people all around me.

I was so mad at the U.S. Marshals when they tore me away from my home. I was a pawn in their game, and I knew it. They knew it too, but on the level that someone carelessly stepping on ants as they walk knows it. It didn't matter. I didn't matter to them. I was an ant to them. Just a consequence and a tool for them to use. If a life—my life—had to be sacrificed so that a group of bad guys could be brought to justice, well, in their eyes that was a sacrifice they would make willingly.

But it was *my* life. *Is* my life? No, was. It was a different life.

When I got here, I hit the reset button.

When I got here I was so skeptical and angry and broody. Superior. Snobby, really. I guess as a line of defense maybe. I saw these small town people through different eyes. I thought they were soft and weak. But they're not. They are kind and full of heart. Compassion.

Maybe I can find faith in the world again.

Maybe I don't have to be invisible the rest of my life.

Maybe I can love.

When I got here, I hit the reset button, but I never let go. I never fully reset. I erased the old but didn't allow for the new.

I became a nothing.

I'm ready to be a someone.

I'm ready to let go.

It's a risk, sure, to date. It's a risk to love. It's a risk to let this guy see me, even knowing I can't let him see my whole heart.

Better to take risks and live fully than never to live at all.

I've been all but dead to the world for the last three years. But guess what?

I'm still alive.

It's time to live again.

TWENTY-FIVE

Megan was still lying in bed reading Bridget's journals when the buzz of an incoming text jarred her back to reality. On seeing that it was from Max, her heart flipped. She smiled groggily, remembering the previous night. Why didn't she go dancing more often? She'd had so much fun. Sure, neither of them would win any dance awards, but they'd had an amazing time, laughing, being silly, making up crazy moves.

"Definitely something to do again soon," Megan said to her phone as she clicked on the green app icon.

Max's message was long.

Had a great time last night. Thank you. Hope I'm not waking you this morning. Hopefully you sleep with do not disturb on. Anyway, got back some news from the lab. Overdose.

Megan frowned. Overdose? That seemed so unlikely.

They think Bridget killed herself? Megan wrote.

No, no, Max wrote back quickly. *Overdose as cause of death, but whether it was intentional on her part, accidental, or via someone else is still being investigated.*

Investigated by the FBI agent, Megan knew. She wondered if Max—and therefore she, herself—would be completely cut out of the process.

Did they say what drug? Megan asked.

Fentanyl, Max wrote back. *Bad stuff.*

Fentanyl, Megan wrote. *What does it look like? Could that be what Lily saw in Simon's backpack?*

What did she see again? Max wrote.

Baggies of white stuff, I think, Megan said. *But I don't know if Lily dug around much. There could have been more.*

I hope she didn't, Max wrote. *Fentanyl in its pure form is dangerous stuff. Some officers have had symptoms just from being around it. Tell Lily to keep away from that backpack.*

I will, Megan wrote. *Also …*

… Yes? Max wrote.

Also, do you know if they tested for propofol? Megan asked.

Propofol? Max said. *That's a new one to me.*

It's just a thought, Megan said. *Propofol is used by anesthesiologists, and we happen to have an anesthesiologist in town right now. Giles. It doesn't last long but it could knock someone out long enough for them to, say, kill them with fentanyl. For example.*

Did you let autocorrect fill out anesthesiologists or did you know how to spell that yourself? Max wrote.

It's possible I could spell anesthesiologist by myself, Megan wrote.

Probably, Max wrote. *You are pretty good at many things.*

Maybe not dancing, Megan wrote, laughing.

Especially dancing, Max wrote.

Megan smiled to herself. Definitely there would be more dancing in the future.

Back to Bridget, she wrote. *I've been reading more in her journals, and I just don't feel like she would kill herself. Or, to be honest, that she'd even do drugs. It seems like she was turning her life around rather than feeling like she needed to end it. So tell those investigators to look into this. Oh, also, there may have been a boyfriend. A new manager at the hotel she used to work at. I'm going to call them this morning once I'm up and ready to go.*

Great, wrote Max. *Keep me updated. And as for the journals ... Agent Silva does want them. Sorry. I'll try to buy you a little time by distracting him, but FYI. Read fast.*

Ahhh drat, Megan wrote. *Okay, thanks for the heads up.*

Gotta go, Max wrote. *Keep up the good work. Thanks again for a fun night. I need more of that.*

Same, Megan wrote. *Anytime.*

She watched her screen for a few moments. Seeing no indication that Max was writing back, she clicked off her phone and put it on her bedside table.

Bridget's notebooks were all spread out on Megan's bed. She looked at them, wishing she could absorb what was inside them just by staring at them. She didn't want to give them up but she knew the choice was not hers.

Megan checked the time: just past seven-thirty. She wanted to call the hotel where Bridget had worked, and she wanted to check in with Lily about Simon, and more than either of those things, with the sun rising on a beautiful day, she wanted to go for a walk.

She started with the hotel. Megan thought she remembered which one Bridget had worked at, but the easiest way to find out was to call. The problem being that Human Resources probably wouldn't be there on a Sunday, much less early on a Sunday morning. But she'd find out what she could.

On the fifth ring, someone at the front desk picked up.

"Hi, this is Megan Montaigne in Emerson Falls," Megan said. "I'm working with the police on a case."

"Oh! A case!" said the woman at the desk dramatically. "Is it about Bridget? We've all been talking about her! Poor thing! I had just started working here right when she left the hotel but she seemed so nice."

"Yes," Megan said. "I'm afraid so. I'm wondering, actually, if I can speak to a manager. A specific one. This would be a man, probably young but I'm not sure, maybe twenty or thirty, light brown hair, who started working there not too long after Bridget left."

"Hmmm," said the woman, thinking. "Well, probably that's Thomas Harrington. He's been out of town for a few days, but I think he's scheduled to be back in this afternoon. Can you hold?"

"Sure," Megan said. The hold music was sharp and brassy, like someone had taken normal music and then put it through a shredder to make it as painful on the ears as possible. Megan held the phone slightly away from her head, just close enough that she'd be able to hear when the woman returned.

After a few minutes, the hold music stopped and the woman's voice came on the line again. "Yes, that's almost certainly Thomas, my co-workers agree. He'll be in at noon. Do you want me to have him call you?"

"I'll try to come by," Megan said. "If you can let him know to expect me. But if he needs to contact me, I'll give you my number." She waited for the woman to find a piece of paper, then passed on her cell phone number and hung up.

Megan checked the time again. Why was it so early? She needed people to be around, to be at their jobs, to be ready to take calls and ask questions.

"A walk," Megan said to the room. She'd just read an article about how walking promotes creative ideas. Maybe a good walk would help her see things more clearly.

She had her walking shoes on and was out the door in minutes, speed walking along the riverside trail. Wondering again, as she had so often, how many people had walked that trail before her. She was agitated, her mind going a million miles per hour, and it took several minutes of brisk walking before she started to feel calm. She slowed her pace just before the spot where she'd seen the lynx. The memory made her walk more quietly. A spotting of a Canada lynx in the wild, this far west and south, was rare. To see it again would be a miracle. Still, she hoped. Walking slowly, she let her eyes relax so they might catch the slightest movement in the shadows. Her breathing slowed to match her pace. It was times like this that she felt like she was part of the Earth; like she was breathing in time with the planet. It was times like this that she could believe everything was connected. Herself, the lynx, Bridget, the past, the future, all of it.

And then, there in front of Addie's bench, she saw it.

Not the lynx.

The caramel crow.

Megan gasped. Since Betty and Carol had mentioned the leucistic crow, Megan had done some research on leucism. The condition wasn't limited to birds; far from it. Megan had seen pictures of leucistic eagles, penguins, peacocks, hummingbirds, bats, owls, and other birds, but also lions, alligators, bears, turtles, giraffes, snakes, horses, deer, squirrels, dolphins, seals …

Every creature on earth.

Each one, born different in a way that to humans was beautiful and special, but to their own species might signify weakness and cause them to be shunned or even killed.

Megan remembered her first conversation with Lester. How he'd talked about what it was like to feel he didn't belong.

And wasn't that it? The thing most people wanted more than anything else.

To know they belonged.

Megan's heart suddenly ached, thinking of the last journal entry she'd read. Bridget had finally found the courage to live again, to risk, to trust, to love. And only weeks later, she was dead.

The caramel crow had found something on the ground to eat, and was only marginally concerned with Megan's presence. Megan stood and watched it. It was so calm, so unconcerned with any chaos and death it had brought forth by being here. Was that the way with any of us? People all going about their lives, clueless as to the destruction left in their wakes. Each just trying to survive.

Megan heard a scuff of a shoe on the trail behind her. She turned to see Giles standing there. She put a finger to her lips, then pointed to the crow. Giles's eyes lit up.

The two of them stood in complete silence for several minutes, thrilled to simply watch the crow exist. Then the crow hopped a few steps and flew away.

"Beautiful," Megan said in a hushed voice, as though speaking in a sacred space.

"It was gorgeous," Giles said, still smiling. "Candace will be sad she missed it."

Something about his tone made Megan think Giles was not particularly concerned with whether Candace would actually be sad.

Suddenly the spell of the caramel crow broke and Megan remembered: this man was one of the last people to have seen Bridget, and he had access to propofol, as well as other drugs. And she had questions.

"Come," she said, walking toward the bench. "It's a beautiful morning. Sit with me?" She sat, and Giles joined her.

"Pretty town you have," he said, his eyes watching the water without focus.

"Except for the murder," Megan said.

The light in Giles's face dropped. "Except for the murder," he said somberly.

Megan sighed and decided to dive in carefully. "She was a nice woman," Megan said. "We'll miss her." She knew Giles had met her. Would he admit it?

Giles nodded. "I'm sure," he said.

No bite, Megan thought. She tried again.

"She worked at the theater. You went to the show didn't you? *The Sound of Music*?" Megan said.

Giles nodded again but said nothing.

Megan decided to try silence as a way of drawing a person out. The two sat for a while, watching the gentle morning breeze as the sun rose higher in the sky, coloring the leaves and the river with its golden light. Neither spoke.

Finally, Megan tried again. "I'm trying to piece together what happened that night. Did you happen to see Bridget?" she said.

Giles's eyelids appeared heavy as he blinked slowly. He turned to Megan with a small smile. "Why do I get the feeling you already know I did?"

"I don't know for sure. Someone matching your description was seen talking to her. The night of the dress rehearsal and the night of her death. I'm wondering if that was you."

Giles looked toward the sky, in the direction the caramel crow had flown off. "Could have been," he said.

"Could have been?" Megan said. "What do you mean? Are you saying you aren't sure if you met her?"

Giles laughed. "What I'm saying, young lady, is that I don't know who your witness saw. It could have been me, because yes, I was there, and yes, I talked to Bridget."

Megan let out a breath. "Did you know her? Before you came here, I mean? Had you met her through Lester?"

A squirrel raced out of the bushes toward them, stopping abruptly to stare at them. Undoubtedly it had seen people here before, and undoubtedly some of them had fed it. It looked at them with huge black eyes and waited, assessing. Were these people going to feed it? When the squirrel determined they were not, it moved on.

Giles rubbed the smooth wood of the bench in what seemed to Megan to be a self-soothing gesture. "I had met her," he said. "Not through Lester. I met her here."

"Here, Emerson Falls?" Megan said.

"Here, at this park in Emerson Falls," Giles said. He bit his lips. "I don't know why I was drawn to her. There was something about her. She was different." He paused, rubbed his palm against the cloth of his trousers. "She was willing to talk to me."

"What did you talk about?" Megan said.

"Birds," he said. "I told her I was here looking for a leucistic crow. She knew what that was. Not a lot of people know. But she knew." He picked a small piece of bark from the bench seat and tossed it to the ground. "Not a lot of people know."

"So you talked about birds?" Megan said.

"Just birds," he said. "But then I wanted to see her again. So I went to the dress rehearsal at the theater on Thursday. I know it was … uncalled for. I didn't mean any harm. I just wanted to be around someone who didn't hate talking to me."

Megan studied the man. He hadn't aged as well as Lester, but he hadn't done too badly. His eyebrows were a bit unruly, but when he smiled, the smile felt genuine. But she knew looks could be deceiving.

"Do you have access to drugs?" Megan asked. "You're an anesthesiologist, right? Were?"

Giles shrugged. "I used to have access, sure. But not anymore. I mean, if I really wanted some, I could get some." He took a breath and seemed to be weighing a decision. "If you really want to know about drugs, you should ask my wife," he said.

"Candace?" Megan said. "Does she have access to drugs?"

Giles looked away. "Do you know what a strange position it is to be in? To be married to someone you realize you can't trust?

To know you're inextricably linked to a person you can't trust. You should talk to her. After the show, when I was down at the party, she went back upstairs to get her jacket." He stood. "Her son is in prison for drugs," he said. "And I won't say any more on that." He looked again to the sky. "One thing I have realized is that regardless of what happens to Candace, I need a divorce. Life is too short to be married to someone who doesn't love you."

The sun was shining behind Giles's head, creating a halo around his body. Megan squinted to look at him. "Do you think your wife could have killed Bridget?" Megan asked.

"I think my wife is capable of pretty much anything," Giles said. "Except love." He turned and walked away.

TWENTY-SIX

No longer in a mood to continue her walk, Megan raced home. Along the way she tapped out a text to Lily.

What do you think of Candace Levine? Possibly capable of killing someone? I just was chatting with her husband. No love lost there at all. He basically accused her. Or Simon? Seems Bridget died of an overdose. Did he ever say anything about the backpack?

Lily didn't text back immediately. It was breakfast time and Megan figured Lily would be busy delighting her guests with perfect eggs Benedict and fluffy Dutch babies, savory quiche Lorraine and sweet streusel-topped coffee cake. "One of these days I need to stay there just for the breakfast," Megan said to her front door as she let herself in.

By the time Megan stepped out of her shower, Lily had sent a signature stream of texts.

Megan!
OMG!
Simon is gone!
Just gone!

Left cash on the pillow in his room and left in the middle of the night!

Backpack is gone too!

Candace, I don't know

She's a weird one

Cold

Definitely no love lost between her and her husband

She glares at him when she thinks he's not looking

Wouldn't tell her my secrets for sure

Hello?

Are you there?

Where are you?

Megan wrapped her long hair in a towel and put on a bathrobe, then sat cross-legged on her bed to text back.

Simon is gone?!? Don't touch the cash. Did you touch it already? Bridget died of fentanyl overdose. Max says it's dangerous in its purest form. Super dangerous. Did you already touch it?

A few moments later, Lily wrote again.

Oh Megan!

I touched it!

Should I get to the hospital?

Now I'm scared!

Megan took a deep breath. *How long ago did you handle it?* she asked.

Two hours ago, Lily wrote.

I walked by his room and the door was open

I looked in the room was empty

So I poked my head in further

All his stuff was gone

Megan considered this a moment.

I haven't had a chance to research fentanyl yet, she wrote, *but I think it would act faster than that if you came in contact. I think you're okay. Just stay aware of how you're feeling and if you start to feel funky, have Steve take you to the hospital. I'm sure you're fine. Have you cleaned the room yet?*

Lily replied immediately.

Oh geez

I hadn't

Do you think I should wait?

Megan inhaled. When calm-cool-collected Lily was panicking, things were bad. Megan would have to step up and be the soothing influence this time.

I think you should text Max, Megan wrote. *Explain what's up. He'll want to know all of it. For now, I'd shut off Simon's room until Max has had a chance to look it over if he wants to. You're fine, Lily. If you're not feeling ill already I'm sure you're fine. Take deep breaths. It's all okay. And keep me updated. Okay?*

Megan could almost feel Lily, a mile away, taking deep breaths. As if once again, like back at Addie's Park, she were connected to the whole universe. She knew instinctively that Lily was actively calming herself down.

Okay, Lily wrote.

I am fine.

I will keep you in the loop.

Love you.

Love you, too, Megan wrote.

She stared at her phone for a few minutes without seeing it. Lily was okay. She was definitely going to be okay. Megan tapped the browser app on her phone and clicked on the search bar. *What are the symptoms of fentanyl exposure?* "Always a good idea to self-diagnose with the internet," she mumbled sarcastically to herself as she hit the submit button. A stream of search results came up and Megan clicked on one that looked promising. The site explained that to overdose on fentanyl, the drug must come into direct contact with mucous membranes or the bloodstream. Reports such as the one Max had told her, about

police having symptoms of fentanyl exposure from merely being in the room with the drugs, were more likely the result of
panic or anxiety. After all, the page said, dealers dealt with the
drugs all the time without dying.

Megan clicked off her phone. The site may or may not be accurate, but she thought it was better not to scare herself any
further.

Still. If that was true, then a casual brush with the drug
couldn't have killed Bridget. Had she taken it willingly? Had
someone slipped it to her in a drink? Megan's mind went once
again to the propofol. And to Candace.

Candace's son was in prison for drugs.

Candace was from Tucson.

Bridget-as-Branwen had lived in Tucson.

Branwen had been involved with a man who was killed for
being part of a drug conspiracy.

Had Candace's son known Simon?

Had Candace and Simon been in on everything together?

Megan's phone buzzed again. This time the incoming text was
from Max.

Just off the phone with Lily, he wrote. *I applied for a search
warrant yesterday but the judge is golfing this weekend. Damn
it! I reassured her she's fine. FYI Agent Silva wants the journals
NOW. I'm bringing him over in fifteen minutes if you're around?*

Megan sighed heavily. She hated to part with the journals.
What was in there that she hadn't had time to learn?

I'm here, Megan wrote. *See you in fifteen.*

She quickly dried her hair and threw on some clothes. Her
hair was still damp when she rushed to the door to let Max and
Agent Silva into the building. Racing back to her bedroom she
gathered up the journals from her bed and put them in the bag
Max had brought them in. She had barely made it back to the
front door when there was a knock from the other side.

"Hey," she said, opening the door to Max's apologetic face. The events of the night before came rushing back into her mind. The dancing. The twinkly lights. The way they'd left things: a short goodbye with a long, lingering look, nothing more.

"Hey," Max said. His eyes hung on hers for a second, then he cleared his throat. "Megan Montaigne, Agent Silva."

Megan stuck out her hand to the tall, thin man, who brought to mind the word "beanpole." A beanpole with glasses. Clothes that fit just right and yet somehow made the agent look like he was dressed up in his father's suit. Younger than Megan had expected, but not less stern. "Nice to meet you, Agent," she said. "Do you want to come in and discuss the case? I've been talking with people and—"

"No need to discuss it," Agent Silva said curtly. "Do you have the journals?" He looked at the bag Megan was carrying in her arms.

"Oh, yes," Megan said, slightly flustered by Agent Silva's lack of interest in polite small talk. She held out the bag. "Here you go. I've been reading and—"

"We will have our people read it, thank you for your service Ms. Montana."

"Montaigne," Max said quietly.

Megan suppressed a smile. It made her happy, somehow, that Max cared to correct the agent.

"Okay, then," Megan said. "Well, if you need anything…."

"Yes, thank you," said Agent Silva. The agent then turned and walked away back to the elevator, clearly assuming Max would follow.

"I'll call you," Max mouthed, holding his hand with his thumb at his ear and pinky finger toward his mouth.

Megan nodded, but her heart fell. Was this it? Was she off the case?

The answer immediately came to her.

No, she was not off the case. She may not be *on* the case officially, but there was nothing illegal about going around asking people questions. Not technically.

She looked at the clock. Just enough time to head down to the theater. And then, off to meet the boyfriend.

Agent Silva could lead his investigation. But this was her town. In some sense, Megan felt a responsibility to the Branwen who had come to Emerson Falls in hopes of a new life, and to the Bridget who had lived there. Bridget might be gone, but she and her story now were a part of the history of the town. Megan would leave no stone unturned.

TWENTY-SEVEN

Megan couldn't imagine there would be too many more undis-covered answers at the theater, but she wanted to talk to Tatum about Simon. She poked her head into the theater at ten o'clock, but no one was there yet, so she headed to the library to work, even though it was Sunday and the library was not open. She was far too restless and needed something to occupy her mind.

With a surge of adrenaline driving her, Megan whipped through all the paperwork that had stacked up. Shortly after eleven o'clock she looked around the library trying to think what else she could do. She tidied for a bit, then went downstairs to see if Owen might be there by some chance, but of course he was not. Megan smiled to herself on remembering Parker. See-ing Owen happy made her happy.

"Maybe I should have Owen and Parker over for dinner," Me-gan said to Owen's empty chair. It would be easy to let someone's death affect her for a few days, let her make promises to herself for a few days about *carpe diem* and reaching out to people she cared about more often, but she hoped very much she wouldn't forget so easily.

Megan glanced over to where the party had been raging two nights before. The door that led to the theater area caught her eye. The police would have been over everything, but no one was perfect. Maybe walking those hallways would spark an insight.

Using the keypad, Megan let herself into the dark hallway and flipped on the lights. Aside from the rooms and shelves full of storage, there wouldn't be much down here, she thought. But someone could have hidden in the basement until the party was underway, waiting either to make their escape or to go upstairs and kill Bridget. Megan let her eyes scan the room loosely for anything that might seem out of place, but she found nothing.

She wandered the hallway toward the stairs that led to the main floor of the theater. Upstairs, she heard a few voices. The crew must be arriving for the day, she thought. When she reached the office area, Megan heard the deep rumble of men's voices coming from the same place she'd overheard Jace talking to Bridget.

This time, one of the speakers was again Jace; the other was Agent Silva. On seeing Megan, Jace looked mildly amused. Agent Silva looked annoyed. Both stopped talking and stared at her.

"Miss Montana," Agent Silva said.

"Montaigne," Megan said, rolling her eyes internally.

"Can we help you?" Agent Silva asked tersely, folding his arms over his chest.

Megan wished for a moment that she'd stopped to eavesdrop. Then she might have a clue what the two were talking about. It was clear she wasn't going to find out now.

"I was just—" Megan pointed back toward the hallways. "Just looking around."

"For clues?" Agent Silva said, raising a disapproving eyebrow.

"Well, I mean … sort of," Megan said.

Agent Silva sighed like a headmaster who had corrected his student too many times. "Miss Montana. Your assistance is no longer needed," he said.

Behind him, Jace shrugged.

"Oh, I know, I was just—" Megan protested.

"The FBI has taken over this case," Agent Silva said.

Megan blinked. She did not care for Agent Silva. Of course he was only doing his job. But was there so much harm in her looking around?

"Yes, I know," Megan said.

"You're dismissed," Agent Silva said.

Megan bit her lips to keep herself from saying what she was thinking. *Dismissed?* Who did he think he was? He had no authority over her. She didn't serve him. She—

She took a deep breath and nodded, and then headed out to the main part of the theater. No point in antagonizing the agent. Maybe he would find out something she hadn't.

Megan was nonetheless still grumbling some choice words to herself, words she wished she'd used with Agent Silva, when she almost bumped right into a person coming down the stairs off the stage.

"Oh!" Megan said, startled. "Sorry!" She looked up. Standing there, blue hair in pigtails and wound around in buns at the sides of her head, was Tatum. "Tatum! You're just the person I wanted to see."

Tatum's expression seemed to be a cross between annoyance and curiosity, pleasure at having been sought out but displeasure that it was Megan doing the seeking. "What did you want?"

"Can we sit?" Megan said, pointing to the front row of chairs. "Do you have time?"

Tatum looked up at the wall, as if toward an invisible clock. "I have a few minutes," she said.

People's curiosity was a wonderful thing, Megan thought. Tatum didn't seem particularly keen on talking, but she clearly wanted to know what Megan wanted.

They sat in the front row of seats, one seat between them, and Megan marveled again at what a lovely job the builders had done. One day these chairs would be old and worn, but for now they were plush and comfortable. She ran her hand over the seat back of the chair that separated her from Tatum. "You have such a nice place to work in," Megan said. "I just love this theater."

Tatum smirked, and Megan thought perhaps Tatum was too cool to admit that she loved anything at all.

"What do you want?" Tatum said.

Internally, Megan sighed. Every time Megan had seen her, Tatum was wearing fifteen layers of defensiveness and distrust, covered by a straight jacket of bravado. Megan wondered if Tatum trusted anyone enough to ever let her guard down; if she ever trusted her own worth enough to just be herself. The weight of all those layers was too heavy to bear.

"I'm wondering what you can tell me about Simon. He seems to have disappeared and we still have questions." A twinge of guilt ran through Megan's mind. But she hadn't said that she was officially investigating. She'd said she still had questions. If Tatum extrapolated from that something other than what Megan meant, well, that was on Tatum.

"He's gone?" Tatum said, the tiniest look of disappointment breaking through her tough veneer.

Megan nodded sadly. "Yeah. Sorry. He didn't tell you?"

Tatum blinked a few times and looked to the stage. "Why would he tell me?" Her walls were rebuilt quickly.

"I thought you and he had spent some time together?" Megan said. "He seemed to like you," she added, hoping that would soften Tatum up.

Her words seemed to have the desired effect as Tatum smiled slightly. "He was all right," she said.

"What do you know about him?" Megan said. "Did you guys talk much?"

Tatum blushed ever so slightly and shrugged a shoulder. "Yeah a little," she said. "Smart guy. He's got big dreams."

"Oh?" Megan said. "Tell me more about that?"

"He wants to have a big house one day on the coast of Spain. A villa with one of those pools, where it looks like it just drops off into the air." Tatum looked to Megan to see if she knew what kind of pool she was talking about.

"An infinity pool?" Megan suggested.

"Yeah, that. An infinity pool. He wants to have a villa in Spain, and then go out to where they dig stuff up. Old stuff." Tatum didn't look at Megan this time but seemed to be pausing to allow Megan to fill in the right words.

"An archaeological dig?" Megan said. "He wants to go out to sites where they uncover the past?"

"Yeah," Tatum smiled. "He said when he was a kid he'd dig in his backyard trying to find dinosaur bones. One day his older brother hid dog bones and Simon got all excited. Then his brother and his dad made fun of him for falling for it." The smile left Tatum's face, like she, too, knew what it was like to have someone mock her and her dreams.

"That sounds like a great dream. Spain, and the pool, and the dig," Megan said.

"He said I could come join him if I wanted," Tatum said. "But I guess not if he's skipped out." She frowned.

"What kind of work did he do?" Megan asked. "Was he, you know, saving money to be able to buy the villa?"

"Pharmaceutical sales," Tatum said, but the return of her smirk suggested the phrase actually meant something else.

"Do you mean he was a drug dealer?" Megan asked. She was

relieved, honestly, that he was gone. She'd been worried about Lily. Maybe Simon did know Lily had gone through his things, but he'd left, and he'd left without hurting anyone. Or, Megan corrected herself, at least without hurting Lily.

Tatum shrugged. "I guess maybe," she said.

"Did he have drugs with him, Tatum?" Megan asked. "Did he offer any to you?" Megan had no idea whether Tatum did drugs of any kind, but it seemed the young woman might get less defensive if Megan put the responsibility on Simon instead.

Tatum let out a heavy sigh of frustration. "Yeah," she said. She opened her mouth to say more, but then closed it again.

"Do you know what kind of drugs he had?" Megan said.

Tatum looked straight at Megan. "Is this about Bridget?" she said. "Is that why you're asking?"

Megan paused. "Well, it's about a lot of things," she said, skirting the answer. "Bridget in part, but not just that."

"Is he going to get in trouble?" Tatum asked.

"Do you think he should get in trouble?" Megan asked.

Tatum laughed lightly. "Yeah," she said. "Probably."

"That wasn't too nice of him to leave without saying anything to you," Megan said softly.

"Nope," Tatum said. Megan thought she saw a tiny glimmer of wetness in Tatum's eyes.

"So do you know what kind of drugs?" Megan asked again. In her mind she wondered what time it was. Was Thomas Harrington at the hotel by now? Megan didn't want to miss him.

"A couple of 'em," Tatum said. "Soft and hard. That's what he told me."

"Hard like cocaine? Heroin? Fentanyl?" Megan asked, trying not to lead too much.

"He might have mentioned coke and fentanyl." Tatum shrugged.

"Okay," Megan said. The fentanyl or cocaine would have been what Lily had seen. "He was selling all of it?"

"Well, we smoked some weed," Tatum admitted. "But it's legal, you know."

"Oh, I know," Megan said. Marijuana had been legalized in the state not too long before. Whether it was fully legal in all instances, whether a person had to have permits to sell it, Megan had no clue. It wasn't the weed she was worried about. "So … I mean, Simon didn't give any indication where he was going next?" Megan made a mental note to herself to check with the auto shop to see whether Simon had simply dumped his car. If he hadn't, then how had he gotten out of town? Bus? Taxi? Hitchhiking?

"Um, no," Tatum said, rolling her eyes. "I didn't know he was leaving. So he didn't say where he was going."

"But there were no clues?" Megan said. "No hints at his plans for the near future?"

Tatum shrugged and huffed a bit, and Megan knew this interview would soon be over. "Like, Canada, maybe," she said. "He said something about Vancouver, but not like 'I'm going to go to Vancouver next to sell my drugs.'" Tatum rolled her eyes again in case Megan hadn't been clear on what a moron she was being.

"Okay. So one last question. Did he seem to know Bridget? Did he say anything about her, ask about her, anything like that?" Megan said.

"That's more than one question," Tatum said, raising an eyebrow.

"Humor me," Megan said.

Tatum looked up to the stage where people were gathering. "Yeah, he asked about her, after she died. He asked if people knew how she died."

"What did you tell him?" Megan asked.

"I told him I'm not a police officer," Tatum said, still staring at the stage.

"Did he seem overly interested in Bridget?" Megan asked. "Like, more curious than your average person would be about a person they didn't know?"

Tatum stood. "Everyone was always overly interested in Bridget," she said. "But now she's gone."

Tatum's smile was a little too bright and for a moment, Megan's mind flipped again. Tatum? Here there was evidence that Tatum had access to fentanyl as well. If she'd been with Simon in his room, she could have easily grabbed a bag out of the backpack. Or bought one. Or Simon could have just given her some. Tatum certainly didn't seem all that sorry Bridget was gone. Could she …?

"I gotta go," Tatum said, and she left.

Everyone was always overly interested in Bridget. The words rang in Megan's head. Of all the things she'd learned, this seemed the most consistently true. Bridget had been a center around which so many events and people had converged, and now she was gone.

TWENTY-EIGHT

The hotel where Bridget had worked looked like any of thousands of other hotels in cities throughout the country, from the covered temporary parking area where people could check in and unload their cars to the vast rows of windows that all looked exactly the same. Even if she hadn't been there before, Megan could predict what she'd find inside: a front desk with a plastic container that would hold hot cookies in the evening; a breakfast area that from somewhere around six a.m. to nine a.m. would serve do-it-yourself waffles, too-dry cinnamon rolls, too-greasy sausage, an assortment of yogurts, and some bananas that looked like they'd fallen off the truck at some point. In the bedrooms there would be a coffee pot no one ever used, and a random strip of fabric at the foot of the bed that was meant to keep the dirt of people's luggage off the bedspread, but which no one ever knew quite what to do with. Leave it on the bed? Drape it over the chair in the corner? And yet, Megan still loved hotels. Being in a hotel meant she was going somewhere, doing something, discovering some new place.

The woman at the front desk gave Megan a professional hotel smile when she walked up. "Checking in?" she said.

"Actually, no," Megan said. "I was told Thomas Harrington would be returning to work at noon today." Megan double-checked the clock on the wall. It was just past twelve-thirty; hopefully she'd given the man enough time to settle in.

"You have an appointment?" the woman said with tired cheerfulness.

"Well, no. But if you could let him know it's about Bridget," Megan said.

The woman's mouth formed into a silent O and she held up a finger indicating "wait one moment." She disappeared behind a door, then reappeared a few minutes later, followed by a man in his late twenties or early thirties.

"You're here about Bridget?" the man said without any preamble. His eyes were not red but the skin of his eyelids seemed a bit puffy, and he was looking at Megan with a mixture of sadness, curiosity, anger, and exhaustion.

"Yes," said Megan. "I'm Megan Montaigne. From Emerson Falls. You're Thomas Harrington?" He nodded. Megan looked around. "Is there somewhere private we can go to talk?"

Thomas seemed to be in a daze, and he took a while to think. "Out back," he said, and he led the way through the lobby, past the indoor swimming pool in its glass cage, and out the door to a large and surprisingly lovely patio area. Past the edge of the patio, evergreen trees towered overhead. Thomas wiped pine needles off a seat and offered the chair to Megan, then did the same for a second chair and sat down.

"How can I help you?" Thomas said. His voice was full of emotion and weariness.

"I'm so sorry for your loss," Megan said. "I've been ... I've been trying to figure out what happened. I think Bridget deserves that."

For a moment Megan thought Thomas was going to burst into tears, but he swallowed hard and pressed his lips together.

"She deserves that," he said.

"You met when she came in to get her paycheck?" Megan said. "Is that right?"

"Yeah," he said, a tiny smile of memory lighting his eyes. "She told me to ask her out."

Megan laughed. "Sounds like she was pretty direct."

"She was both," Thomas said. "Pretty. And direct." His eyes glistened and he looked up to the top of the trees.

"Did she ever mention … a past? Trouble? Anything?" Megan asked.

Thomas picked up a pine needle from the tabletop and started breaking it apart. "I've been hearing these things," he said. "Rumors are going around. But …" he looked into Megan's eyes, almost a plea. "I didn't know anything. Do you know? Can you tell me?"

Megan inhaled deeply and sighed. "I don't know all of it," she said. "It seems she was in the witness protection program. A drug conspiracy, a drug ring, whatever they call it. They—" Megan took a breath. "They murdered her boyfriend in front of her, and she was called to testify. I think she was done with the testimony, actually, but yet …"

Thomas buried his face in his hands. His shoulders shook. After a few moments, he looked up, his eyes wet. "I mean, we'd just started dating. I don't know why I'm so upset."

"Because it's upsetting," Megan said. "Because you cared."

"I didn't know any of that," Thomas said. "She never said a word. She seemed so happy."

"Well," Megan said. "We don't even know yet that it was someone from the drug ring who killed her. It could have been anyone." What a horrible idea, Megan thought, that her killer could have been anyone Bridget knew. "Do you know, did she have any troubles here in Emerson Falls? Any enemies? Any old flames or jealous competition? Did she have conflict at work, with a landlord, anything?"

Thomas rubbed his eyes, thinking. "Nothing outside the ordinary. Nothing I've heard of here at the hotel. I mean—" He stopped.

"Yes?" Megan said encouragingly. She knew that often the thing that seemed least important to someone, but which they nonetheless felt the need to bring up, ended up being critical to the case.

"Well, I didn't work here at the same time Bridget did. But since she left ... since we started dating ... I've occasionally heard people say they didn't like her. They thought she was standoffish. Superiority complex. That kind of thing. Too good to work here, kept to herself, didn't make friends. Which," he took a breath. "Which all makes a little more sense now." He shook his head. "I wish I'd known. I wish she would have told me. I wish she'd trusted me."

"I can't imagine it would have been easy for her to trust," Megan said. "It wasn't just you."

"I know, but ... she needed someone. I wasn't there." His face fell into his hands again. He didn't seem to be sobbing this time, though; just defeated.

"But you don't know anyone specifically who might have wanted to hurt her? No threats or anything?" Megan asked.

Thomas shook his head. "The conflict was all just run-of-the-mill conflict. Nothing that raised any red flags. I'm sorry."

"Don't be sorry," Megan said. "It's not your fault. If you think of anything, though, call me, okay?" She pulled a business card out of her purse and handed it to Thomas. "And don't blame yourself. Although ..."

Thomas looked up. "Although?"

"I guess I should ask you. You were out of town when Bridget was killed? Is that correct?" Megan asked.

Thomas stiffened. "I was at my cabin, yes. Down south, off of Highway 2."

"Were you with anyone?" Megan said uncomfortably. This was so awkward.

"No," Thomas said. "But I went to local restaurants for meals. They'll vouch for me. If the police need that."

"How far of a drive is that?" Megan asked. "From here to your cabin."

Thomas's demeanor was turning cold, but he answered nonetheless. "A little over two hours." He blinked. "When was Bridget killed?"

"After the show on Friday," Megan said. "Sometime between ten and eleven."

Thomas heaved a sigh of relief. "Friday night I was at a restaurant until after nine. So unless I drove exceptionally fast, that should take me off the suspect list. Do you need the name of the restaurant?"

Megan realized that asking for the restaurant name might be pushing it a bit far, since she had been told to stop her sleuthing. The most she could do, really, would be to tell Max, and let him take it from there.

"No," she said. "If the police need it, they'll let you know." She stood. "Again, I'm so sorry for your loss. I've been there. My fiancé died a couple of years ago. If you need someone who understands …" She pointed to her business card.

Thomas nodded, and in the nod Megan could feel she had been dismissed.

"Thank you for your time, Thomas," Megan said.

Back in the lobby, Megan stopped at the front desk again. "Thanks so much," she said to the clerk. She was about to leave when a thought occurred to her, and she turned back. "Say, has anyone been by or called about Bridget? Recently, I mean. Before she died. Someone you didn't know."

The woman thought a moment. "No, I don't think so. Well, wait. I mean there was a guy that stopped by wondering if she still worked here, but when I told him she was working at the theater now, he just left."

"A guy came by looking for her?" Megan said, her heart beating a little faster. "When was this? What did he look like?"

"A few nights ago," the clerk said. "A night or two before Bridget died. It was in the evening. He was, I don't know, average height, dark hair, black leather jacket. Maybe in his twenties? I didn't really pay attention. Sort of a mean-looking guy. I was glad he left, to be honest."

"And you told him Bridget worked in Emerson Falls? At the theater?" Megan said, her breath now feeling very shallow.

"Yeah," the woman said. "Pointed him in the right direction and he left without another word."

Megan's heart was in her throat. "Thanks!" she called back over her shoulder as she rushed out of the hotel.

Dark hair, black leather jacket.

Simon.

TWENTY-NINE

When Megan pulled her car around the back of the library to park, she saw Max standing at the door, apparently looking for her. Quickly parking, she jumped out of her car.

"Max!" she said, almost breathless with excitement. "Max! Simon!"

Max turned and smiled when he saw her. "I was just looking for you," he said.

"Here I am," Megan said, returning his smile. "Max, I was just at the hotel where Bridget used to work. I asked at the front desk—"

But Max had put up his hand in a "stop" motion. "Hang on," he said.

Megan squinted at him. "What?"

Max said nothing.

"What's going on, Max?" Megan pressed.

Max looked around the library grounds. The deciduous trees were starting to change to their fall colors; a Japanese maple planted near the back entrance was midway between its ordinary green and the bright, fiery orange-red it would eventually wear. The breeze that lifted Megan's long hair was warm, but it held within its edges the cool breath of autumn. Change was on the way.

"Let's go down to the benches," Max said.

Megan stared at him. "Max. What?" She put her hands on her hips. "Tell me. What?"

Max sighed heavily. "I know you're not going to like this. Agent Silva … Agent Silva says he has determined Bridget's death to be a suicide. The case is over. We're done investigating."

Megan's mouth dropped open. "Suicide!" she said once she regained her words. "No way, Max. Did he read the journals? He didn't even read them, did he! There's no way. It's impossible. Bridget, or Branwen, or whoever she was, wasn't suicidal. She had just re-found her desire to live. She'd just started dating again. I'm telling you, there is no way she killed herself! And what's more, Simon—"

"Let's go down to the benches?" Max said again. He held out his hand.

Megan took Max's hand and let him lead the way, but her mind was reeling. As soon as they were seated, she started up again. "Max, I was at the hotel. The one where Bridget worked. I asked at the front desk, just on a whim, I asked if anyone had been asking about Bridget. The woman said a guy had come by looking for her. It sounded just like Simon. And it could have been the same night that he showed up in Emerson Falls. Why would Simon ask for Bridget at the hotel and then just happen to show up in Emerson Falls, pretending he'd just broken down coincidentally? Did you check with the auto body shop? They said it could have been staged, the breakdown. Did you ask them?"

"Megan …" Max said.

"And then, I'm just getting started here, Max, then there's

Tatum. She didn't like Bridget. Honestly, I think she hated her. Jealousy, through and through. I could see her doing it. She hooked up with Simon, Simon had fentanyl, Tatum got pissed off at Bridget for some imagined wrong, and in the heat of the moment she killed her. After all, she was there right after Jace found Bridget, right? Why wasn't Tatum down at the party, too? Why was she upstairs? The cleanup could have been done the next day. There was no reason for her to be upstairs, really. Did Agent Silva investigate that?" The words were flying out of Megan, barely giving Max a chance to respond.

"And for that matter, how much did anyone even talk to Jace? He seems so sketchy, Max. There's something off about him. He shows up here in town and then a few weeks later one of his staff is dead? He never really wanted to talk to me. Someone should follow up with him. Or Giles. Giles could have had access to any number of drugs, I'd guess. I mean how hard would it be for a doctor to get a drug? Fentanyl? And he had very quickly become obsessed with Bridget. Heat of the moment, guy wants woman, woman says no, man kills woman. A tale as old as time. Or Candace. Giles's wife. She had access to all the drugs and her son was in prison for drugs. And she hated Giles, and she might have killed Bridget because Giles was interested in her. Or she might have killed Bridget to get back at Lester. Or she might have killed Bridget because Bridget was somehow involved in her son going to jail. Did Agent Silva look at any of that?"

Max didn't answer. What was there to say?

They sat in silence a while, Megan in fuming disbelief, and Max trying to absorb her anger. The autumn afternoon sunlight glazed the river, hiding everything underneath. Someone in the distance was mowing a lawn. The air was filled with the crisp scent of the water.

"It sucks," Max said finally. "I know you're frustrated."

"There's nothing we can do?" Megan said.

Max shook his head. "FBI. Out of my hands. They say it's done, so it's done."

"But Max," Megan said. "It's not fair. There's no justice there."

Max looked at Megan sadly. "I know."

The walkie talkie clipped to Max's uniform hissed, and a dispatcher came through asking if he was there.

Max looked at Megan. "I've got to go. I'll call you later?"

Megan shrugged and nodded. Max left.

Megan didn't know whether to scream or cry. She was furious. The injustice of it all. She'd only just begun her investigation and now … Who was this Agent Silva anyway? She wanted to report him. She wanted to do more than that to him. Kick him, scream at him, get him to understand that Bridget would never have killed herself. What an incompetent …

She took a deep breath and headed upstairs to her apartment.

But once there, she still couldn't calm herself down.

She looked around her home.

"Time for some rage cleaning," she said to the kitchen, and she got out her steam mop.

Three hours later she was standing outside on the bedroom balcony, shining up the massive windows as if the future of humanity depended on it. Standing on a chair, she scrubbed the dirt from the last dirty corner. Strands of her hair clung to the sweat on her neck. She was exhausted.

When she was done, she climbed slowly off the chair. She looked down at the river and started to cry. But crying would not do, she thought. Megan walked back into her bedroom and let off a primal scream. She started to kick, arresting the kick halfway. The inertia sent her sandal flying over her bed and Megan realized she needed to be careful or she'd knock over a lamp.

Inhale, exhale. Inhale, exhale. After a few deep breaths, Megan walked to get her shoe, which had bounced under the bed. Megan got down on her knees to reach for the sandal.

"Wait," Megan said, staring under the bed. "What is this?"

She felt her heart jump as she realized what she was looking at. One of Bridget's journals.

"I must have knocked it off the bed earlier," she said. Earlier, when she'd been gathering them up for Agent Silva. One of them, this one, must have fallen off the bed without her noticing.

Megan sat back on her heels and opened the journal. The dates were very recent. There were only a few entries, maybe a dozen. This must have been the last journal.

Megan started reading.

Her jaw dropped.

"I am going to need some wine for this," she whispered. She went to the kitchen, poured herself a large glass of wine, took the journal out to the balcony, and read.

THIRTY

The marshal that's been assigned to me, Jace, just contacted me. He said there's word Joel's people are trying hard to track me down. I don't know why. I've testified. It's over. Killing me won't do them any good now.

Revenge. Best served cold, I guess.

I'm scared.

Jace is going to try to get a job in Emerson Falls and try to watch over me and figure out how to move forward but he says we have to be prepared to move fast at any point. I said I'd put in a word for him at the theater but he said no, it's better if people don't realize we know each other.

It's all my fault. I'm going to have to move again and it's all my fault.

I don't know what got into me, sending that rare bird alert. I saw that there was a rare bird at the coast and I just hoped that maybe I could see my dad one more time. I guess I didn't realize anyone would figure it out other than Lester. Or maybe my sub-conscious, that part of me that can see through the veil of time, knew that this might be my last chance to see him. One way or another. Either I'd have to move on, or I'd be dead.

When Lester came, he brought unexpected company. Candace came too, and I think she recognized me. Her son was in jail. That one wasn't my doing but I know she knows the same people. I don't know if she sent word or if the guy came on his own but there's a guy in town that Jace says is here for me. Told people his car broke down. But Jace knows who he is.

Candace had always been bitter toward Lester. She had been jealous of my mother and jealous of me, even. I remember her. Maybe the guy found me on his own or maybe Candace told him but the thing is, he's here.

Jace said we'd have to move fast and we're moving fast. Faked death. He says they've done it before, in rare cases. The whole thing will be staged with marshals. Fake ambulance. Fake EMTs. They'll come in and take me away on a gurney and then Jace will come along and get me to the airport. Later, they'll send fake word to the police officer that I've died. Fake FBI might get involved, or maybe real FBI telling lies, I don't know.

Same story as before. New passport, new papers, new life.

I have to choose a new name tonight.

Goodbye, Emerson Falls.

Megan's phone buzzed. Her wine glass was empty and her head was full.

And now, if she was reading the journal entries right, she knew Bridget was safe.

She looked at her phone: a text from Max.

I feel like sitting at your fire pit with a bottle of wine. Do you want to join me?

Megan looked at her empty glass. What was another bottle among friends?

Yes. Come over. I'll meet you there.

Megan gathered up a couple of old blankets, a couple of wine glasses, and a corkscrew. When she got to the fire pit, Max was already waiting.

"How are you doing?" he asked. He looked deeply into her eyes. Concerned. Wanting to fix things.

"I'm okay," Megan said. "I've come to terms with it. I think Bridget is probably in a better place now." She smiled, imagining Bridget, with her new name, sitting on a bench somewhere, staring at the water, just as she and Max were watching the river flow by.

"You're sure?" Max said. He opened the bottle of wine and poured them each a glass.

"I'm sure," Megan said. She raised her glass. "Here's to life."

"To life," Max said. He held Megan's eyes a while, and then looked away at the water.

The sun fell slowly, not wanting to give up the day, its beams stretching the long shadows out into the evening. Max and Megan shared their thoughts about life, death, and what they would do if they were given a second chance.

Or third, Megan thought.

After a while, Max declared he had to go home.

"Thanks for coming by," Megan said, walking him to his car. "Thanks for checking on me."

"Anytime," Max said. He put his hand on Megan's shoulder for a moment, then got into his car and headed home.

Megan watched the taillights of his car, two red eyes escaping into the dark.

She gathered up the blankets and one wine glass and headed upstairs, leaving her wine glass and the bottle behind.

Bridget's journal was still on the balcony, where Megan had

left it. Megan studied its cover, wondering what Bridget would be writing tonight.

Megan picked up the journal, grabbed some matches, and went back downstairs to the fire pit.

One by one, Megan tore out the pages Bridget had written on and rolled them into paper logs. She put them in the pit and placed a stone on top of them to hold them in place. A small puff of wind blew out the first match so she tried again. Success. She touched the tip of the match to one roll of the paper, then another, and another.

Bridget Hill's last days went up in flames.

Megan slowly ripped the cover off of the remaining pages and fed it into the fire, watching as the red embers grew brighter into flames for a moment before dying down again. She ripped off a few of the blank pages and lay them in the fire. Then a few more pages, and a few more, until all the pages of the journal had been consumed. Megan watched as the pages of the journal transformed into ashy ghosts of their former selves. The remnants of Bridget's second life floated into the air on breaths of wind.

Air.

Megan was water, Max was earth, and Bridget was air. Like her father.

Megan poured the final drops of wine into her glass, and lifted it to the sky with a silent toast: *To Bridget, wherever you may be.*

EPILOGUE

I just got a package. They sent me my journals, but I've just realized one is missing. I'm assuming Jace kept it. Hopefully destroyed it. I wrote down everything in it, all the plans to get me out of Emerson Falls, the whole faking-my-death scheme.

That was stupid. I won't do that again.

You don't get to your third life without learning some things.

From now on, everything I write goes straight into the fireplace. Write and burn.

I read somewhere that on the Galapagos Islands, a new finch species has just recently evolved. In the last few years. While scientists were watching. It had to change; it had to adapt in order to survive, and so it did.

Maybe that's me.

First there was Branwen.

Then there was Bridget.

And now there's Adeline.

Inspired by dear Addie in Emerson Falls. I know, it's not a common name. But I decided I'm not a common person. I'll never fit in. I can only be me.

I know, I remember, yes, I was supposed to pick a name that started with B for when I sign my checks. Jace, ever diligent, reminded me, but I hadn't forgotten. I just wanted a change. And who writes checks anymore? Maybe they need to update that rule.

They've assigned me a new marshal, too. A woman this time. I don't imagine I'll see much of her. There's no need, really. We're all hoping that now that my testimony is over, the damage is done, and I'm supposedly dead, they'll forget. That they won't care anymore. Won't be watching for me anymore. Won't be hiring one of the girlfriends' little brothers who is a computer-hacking wizard to track me down through my completely careless searches of stories about the trial and my stupid cyber-stalking of all the people involved in it.

Whoops.

Anyway, I'm here now.

Act one: Tucson.

Act two: Emerson Falls.

Act three: Sitka, Alaska.

They keep moving me north. If I have to go through this again, I'll be at the North Pole. Maybe I'll find elves.

Honestly, Sitka is really nice. If I thought Emerson Falls was all about water, I was wrong. Sitka is defined by water. It's beautiful and it's everywhere and it feels like being reborn.

I'm going to do it all differently this time. I'm going to do it right this time.

I missed the past too much last time; focused too often on all the things that would never be. I wished too hard for a future that was already lost. And in doing so, I lost the time I had.

What I finally figured out is that life is not about the past or the future. It's about this moment. Right now.

In this moment I'm in the coffee shop and the barista made

my chai tea just right. This is my third time here, and I'm a regular now. The day is cool and misty, with threads of fog hanging out over the water. There's a man at the next table reading something on his laptop and smiling to himself, trying to contain a laugh. There's a woman walking outside with her dog, a black lab. The lab looks happy. I am trying out for a local dance troupe this afternoon and I'm told they take just about anyone who's interested so I think my chances are high. But that's the future too. It's so easy to get lost outside of "now" but now is everything and now is all we ever have.

I've been making a list. Just who is Adeline Brooks?

She's a survivor. She doesn't talk about the past. She is happy. She chooses joy. She lets go. She lets people in. She goes on long walks and she eats organic foods. She dances. She sings, badly, but she sings. She's open to just about anything.

She lives.

I feel like the people of Alaska will let me be me. Live and let live. They don't want me in their business and they're not going to get all up in mine.

So whoever I'm going to be, now's my chance.

The man at the laptop just caught me watching him laugh. He gave me a big smile and a wink.

I may wink back.

That's all we need. A good chai tea, a stranger to make into a friend, and the moment we are in. The past is gone. Live now.

I saw the Northern Lights last night for the first time. I can't even describe them. It's the most impossible thing I've ever seen. It felt like looking into the afterlife or another universe. Like the sky was trying to talk to me.

Like the sky wanted me to know everything is going to be okay.

Like it was telling me that I am finally home.

THE MEGAN MONTAIGNE MYSTERIES

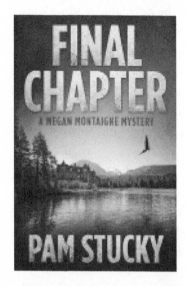

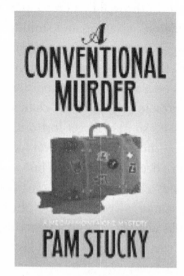

For Megan Montaigne, library director, living in the top floor of the mansion-turned-library is a dream come true. At least it was, before the murders started.

"Superb writing, extraordinary characters. A fantastically well-written novel with characters so real that one might reach out and touch them."

"I loved every page of this novel. Did not want to stop reading and wanted more as I read the last word."

DEATH AT GLACIER LAKE

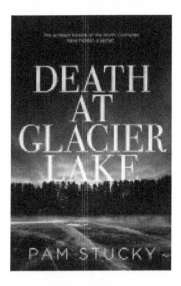

A fast-paced, atmospheric mystery that will keep you guessing until the end!

For two decades, the lush, isolated forests of the North Cascades have hidden a secret. Now, twenty years later, a mysterious contest has brought Mindy Harris back to the area she thought she'd left behind forever. A seemingly innocent creative design firm shows up for a company retreat, but all goes awry when one of their own turns up dead. Was it an accident? Murder? And how does the unsolved mystery from twenty years ago play into it all?

"One of the best Kindle books I have read so far. An unusual ending, love and hate, trust and mistrust, a little of everything. Just like real life. Not a cliff hanger, just a good, stand alone story. Loved every bit of it."

"A neat little mystery with the rare virtue that the setting and characters are as interesting as the unfolding story."

More by Pam Stucky

The Balky Point Adventures (MG/YA sci-fi)

"Aliens, infinite universes, ghosts AND time travel ... a winning literary combination if ever there was one." — Just One More Chapter reviews

This smart and unforgettable middle grade / young adult science fiction adventure series takes teens Emma, Charlie, Eve, and Ben, along with brilliant but quirky Dr. Waldo and a host of others, on adventures through time and space. Inspired the timeless wonder and fantasy of *A Wrinkle in Time*, with just a dash of *Doctor Who*, the Balky Point Adventures are for readers of all ages who love a good romp through the imaginative marvels of the universes, delivered with heart and wonder. Exciting and imaginative, courageous and thought-provoking, this series commends the strength of compassion, and the inherent power within each person to change the world ... or the universe.

Includes: **The Universes Inside the Lighthouse, The Secret of the Dark Galaxy Stone, The Planet of the Memory Thieves.**

The Wishing Rock series (contemporary fiction)

"It was just what the doctor ordered, fresh, quirky, funny in places and seasoned with wisdom. Light without being frivolous, it follows the story of a woman trying to find someone to fill her desire for true love and family." — Tahlia Newland, author

Wishing Rock, Washington, on Dogwinkle Island—don't look for it on a map; you won't find it there. The only place you can find this town is in your heart—and in the books in the Wishing Rock series!

The Wishing Rock books take us to the fictional town of Wishing Rock, in which all the town's residents live in the same building. In this *Northern Exposure*-esque slice-of-life series, letters between the neighbors and their friends chronicle the twists and turns of the characters' daily lives, and are interspersed with recipes tried and tested by the characters themselves. These novels, filled with wit, wisdom, and recipes, take characters on adventures far and near, and ultimately offer up insightful exploration of the ideas of community, relationships, happiness, hope, forgiveness, risk, trust, and love.

Includes: *Letters from Wishing Rock*, *The Wishing Rock Theory of Life*, and *The Tides of Wishing Rock* (all novels with recipes); *From the Wishing Rock Kitchens: Recipes from the Series* completes the series, with a compilation of all the recipes in the first three books.

The Pam on the Map series (travelogues)

"I couldn't resist reading the entire book, both for the wit and chuckles that I found on nearly every page, and to make sure I didn't miss any of the useful tips that were scattered throughout. I'm big on pre-trip research, and I found some tips in this book that I haven't seen elsewhere." — Emily, Amazon reader

In her Pam on the Map series, Pam sets out to discover and connect with people and places, and to take readers along on her adventures through her almost real-time reports. Raw and real, Pam's tales are infused with candid honesty, humorous observations, and perceptive insights. Pam's descriptive, entertaining, conversational style brings her trips alive, making readers feel as though they're traveling right along with her.

Though they're not guidebooks, the Pam on the Map books are still informative and illuminating, providing useful tips and plentiful ideas for people who might want to follow along in Pam's footsteps.

Includes: *Pam on the Map: Iceland, Pam on the Map: Seattle Day Trips, Pam on the Map (Retrospective): Ireland,* and *Pam on the Map (Retrospective): Switzerland.*

ACKNOWLEDGMENTS

Caution: Spoilers ahead!

Here's what I can tell you about the Witness Protection Program: no one will tell you anything about it. I called the U.S. Marshals Service office, who directed me to the U.S. Attorney General's office. In the U.S. Attorney General's office, I talked to the public information office, where a very nice woman told me that when people call with questions, she generally tells them, "Use your imagination." She nonetheless indulged me in my questions, but gave me no answers, telling me that in her office they don't even know the answers to the questions I was asking. I asked my local Police Chief if he knew anything about what local law enforcement would know if there was a witness being protected in their jurisdiction. He didn't know, nor did anyone he asked.

So my point is, I have no idea if any of what I wrote is accurate. The best I could do was to read the fascinating book *WITSEC: Inside the Federal Witness Protection Program*, by investigative journalist Pete Earley and the man who created the Witness Protection Program, Gerald Shur, and then, as suggested, use my imagination.

Thank you also to: Kris Gates and Beth Stucky for insights into birds and birding; the Legal Fiction Facebook group for legal insights; Patrick O'Donnell for police guidance; and Beth Stucky and Donna Hostick for reading early drafts. And to everyone else who travels along with me on the journey, always, thank you.

CONNECT

If you loved this book, tell your friends and let Pam know! Leave a review online, send a tweet to @pamstucky, and/or drop Pam a note at facebook.com/pamstuckyauthor.

Stay tuned for more! Be among the first to know when a new story is coming out by signing up for Pam's mailing list at pamstucky.com!

Visit pamstucky.com to find out more about Pam and her other fiction and non-fiction books.

Made in the USA
Coppell, TX
31 May 2021

56627230R00142